Praise for Aoibheann Sweeney's
Among Other Things, I've Taken Up Smoking

"In Sweeney's modern myth about an island, a city, a daughter, her father, and his books, the world is so freshly minted the steam seems still to be rising from it. Transformation is the order of the day, and finding love is very nearly as painful as the ever-beckoning insularity that is its alternative."　　　　　　　—Alison Bechdel, author of *Fun Home*

"Lovely . . . You don't have to catch the allusions here to *The Tempest*, but part of the novel's considerable charm is how lightly it taps into older, sometimes ancient stories. . . . The pleasure of this novel stems from Sweeney's gentle balance of comedy and sorrow. . . . There's real wisdom in these classic myths and there's real talent in this sensitive novel."　　　　　　　—*The Washington Post Book World*

"*Among Other Things, I've Taken Up Smoking* is a fresh, intriguing perspective on coming of age. . . . [It] is not only intriguing, but likely to entice anyone into what lured Miranda and her father onto Crab Island—'Ovid's spell.'"
　　　　　　　—Jonathan Trumbull, *The Philadelphia Inquirer*

"A poignant mix of loneliness and danger."　　　　　　　—*Chicago Tribune*

"For each of us there will always come a day, a season, a year when we'll step out of the fog and say this is who I am, this is what I want, here I must live. In this magical, wonderful novel that is Shakespeare and Ovid, Wharton and Altman braided in one, a new, thrilled, authentic voice takes us back to our unborn selves—stranded, shapeless, searching for that one thing we aren't too sure we have in us to give: love."
　　—Andre Aciman, author of *Out of Egypt* and *Call Me by Your Name*

"Sweeney's narrative marks itself as 'literary' in all the right ways, with its lovely descriptive passages and subtlety."　　　　—*TimeOut New York*

"Stylish."　　　　—John Freeman, president of the National Book Critics Circle, *The Phoenix*

"Assured, engaging . . . nervy, inspired . . . If Miranda Donnal makes a mistake taking up smoking, you won't regret sinking into this book."
　　　　　　　—Newhouse News Service

PENGUIN BOOKS

AMONG OTHER THINGS,
I'VE TAKEN UP SMOKING

Aoibheann Sweeney earned her BA at Harvard University, where she won the John Harvard scholarship and Elizabeth Carey Agassicz Award and her MFA at the University of Virginia, where she was a Henry Hoynes Fellow. She has been a resident fellow at the MacDowell Colony and at Yaddo. She has written book reviews for the *New York Times Book Review*, the *Washington Post Book World*, and the *Village Voice Literary Supplement*. She is currently director of the Center for the Humanities at The Graduate Center, City University of New York.

Among

other things,

I've taken up

smoking

——

Aoibheann Sweeney

PENGUIN BOOKS

PENGUIN BOOKS

Published by the Penguin Group

Penguin Group (USA) Inc., 375 Hudson Street, New York, New York 10014, U.S.A.
Penguin Group (Canada), 90 Eglinton Avenue East, Suite 700, Toronto, Ontario, Canada M4P
2Y3 (a division of Pearson Penguin Canada Inc.) • Penguin Books Ltd, 80 Strand, London
WC2R 0RL, England • Penguin Ireland, 25 St Stephen's Green, Dublin 2, Ireland (a division
of Penguin Books Ltd) • Penguin Group (Australia), 250 Camberwell Road, Camberwell,
Victoria 3124, Australia (a division of Pearson Australia Group Pty Ltd) • Penguin Books India
Pvt Ltd, 11 Community Centre, Panchsheel Park, New Delhi – 110 017, India • Penguin
Group (NZ), 67 Apollo Drive, Rosedale, North Shore 0632, New Zealand (a division of Pearson
New Zealand Ltd) • Penguin Books (South Africa) (Pty) Ltd, 24 Sturdee Avenue,
Rosebank, Johannesburg 2196, South Africa

Penguin Books Ltd, Registered Offices: 80 Strand, London WC2R 0RL, England

First published in the United States of America by The Penguin Press,
a member of Penguin Group (USA) Inc. 2007
Published in Penguin Books 2008

1 3 5 7 9 10 8 6 4 2

AUTHOR'S NOTE
For my narrations of Ovid's tales I have relied on various translations, including ones by
Mary M. Innes (*Metamorphoses*, Penguin Books, 1955); Frank Justus Miller (*Metamorphoses*,
Loeb Classical Library, Books I–VIII, revised by G. P. Goold, 1977, and *Metamorphoses*,
Loeb Classical Library, Books I–VIII, revised by G. P. Goold, 1984); and
Ted Hughes (*Tales from Ovid*, Farrar Straus and Giroux, 1997).

THE LIBRARY OF CONGRESS HAS CATALOGED THE HARDCOVER EDITION AS FOLLOWS:
Sweeney, Aoibheann.
Among other things, I've taken up smoking / Aoibheann Sweeney.
p. cm.
ISBN 978-1-59420-130-1 (hc.)
ISBN 978-0-14-311341-6 (pbk.)
I. Title.
PS3619.W4425A8 2007
813'.6—dc22 2006039182

Printed in the United States of America
Set in Simoncini Garamond
Designed by Stephanie Huntwork

For my mother and father
who keep on loving each other

Among
other things,
I've taken up
smoking

the age of silver

1

Among other things, I've taken up smoking. Ana says I should stop with the good girl/bad girl stuff, and obviously she's right, but sometimes when I have a cigarette in my hand and the streets are dangerously empty and I've had a few drinks after my shift and I am noticing the lights that are on in different apartments, lighting stairways and whole buildings, blinking red on the skyline, I think about the nights on the island when I was content to stand alone outside the house, listening to the fog horns in that soft blackness, and tasting the air, sweet with salt.

My mother and father moved to Maine when I was almost three, so that my father could work on a translation of Ovid's *Metamorphoses*. I grew up on Crab Island, about a mile or so across the water from a small town called Yvesport, which, more often than not, was hidden from us by a thick Down East fog. A few months after we arrived my mother disappeared into the fog and didn't come back. She cooked us oatmeal in the morning and then went into town. When she didn't return that night my father made more oatmeal and put me to bed; in the morning he radioed Mr. Blackwell, who checked to see if our boat was at the dock. That afternoon the Coast Guard found the boat washed up on the mainland without a scratch. It took them three days to find the drowned body. They asked us lots of questions. Mr. Blackwell told me later that she would have frozen to death before she drowned—in the winter it takes about six minutes for your heart to stop beating. She wasn't used to boats, he said— she must have lost her balance, trying to see her way.

My father didn't talk about her, but Mr. Blackwell came over every day after she was gone to make us lunch and supper. I was convinced that all around the island there were women inside the trees. When the wind was up they whispered and showed the underside of their leaves, and I pretended not to hear them. I remember sitting in the yard for hours during the summer, just listening to my breath, feeling my limbs go numb—watching for twilight when the bats would crisscross between the blackening trees behind the house. Sometimes I could almost feel my skin thickening into bark, my toes rooting into the ground, my arms raising stiffly to the sky. My father would forget I was there, and I would watch him wander over to the window, stand for a long time looking out. I liked to imagine he was looking for me—calling my name. I pictured him stopping in front of the new sapling in the yard, studying me in a way he had never looked at a tree before, trying to see my skinny form underneath the bark. My elbows would be knots in the thin branches of my arms, and finally he would recognize my knobby knees, my flat-chested trunk.

My father is Irish and trained for the priesthood when he was growing up but ended up teaching Latin and Greek, first in Boston and then in New York City, where he helped a man named Arthur Mitchell found the Institute for Classical Studies. He has a picture of himself with Arthur Mitchell on his desk: In it my father is tall and young, his hair inky black. Arthur Mitchell is small and dapper, holding a cane just off the ground, like a walking stick. It was through him that my father inherited the island and the house. Mr. Blackwell told me he still remembers driving my mother and father and me across the water to the island the day we arrived. My mother was carrying two blue suitcases and my father had his duffel bag; the books came later. Mr. Blackwell says he carried me all the way up through the underbrush to the house, holding nettles away from my fat little legs. When my father unlocked the door, we could see the furniture, which had been carefully draped with sheets, was spattered with bird droppings. Mr. Blackwell put me down and walked toward the fireplace to check if the flue had been left open. A huge raccoon came out from behind the couch to hiss and spit at all four of us. My mother screamed. Mr. Blackwell figured the animal was rabid; he picked up the iron hat rack and smashed it in the head. Its skull split open and it made such a bloody mess that my father went outside onto the rickety porch to throw up. I went straight for the dead animal, crouched over it to give it a good long look.

I think I do remember her little hands, curled up like she was sleeping, but the rest—the bloodied head—I don't remember at all. It turned out that she had nested in one corner of a velvet couch near the fireplace and had been protecting five pink babies that were squirming blindly in the stuffing. My father helped Mr. Blackwell bury her, and the two of them carried the ruined couch outside. Later I helped them gather a pile of branches to put on top of the babies to protect them from the eagles, but they were gone the next day, and I suppose there must have been very little chance they would survive.

In the years after my mother was gone Mr. Blackwell looked after me, and I followed him everywhere except fishing. When he went out on trips in the *Sylvia B.* he was gone for weeks at a time, but in those days he was not fishing often. When I was old enough he used the *Sylvia B.* to take me back and forth to Yvesport Elementary School, before he taught me how to drive our dory myself. It occurred to me only later that my father must have paid him all that time. When he finally went back to work full time, fishing for a Canadian company that was still buying herring, I was almost ten. My father gave me his watch and told me to go wherever I wanted as long as I was home on time for us to make dinner.

I started timing things. I timed how long it took to get up to the first branch of the apple tree from the house, how long it took if I started down by the beach, how long it took to get from the porch to the cliffs, how long it took to walk around the island through the woods and how long it took along the shore, balancing on just the big rocks. The watch slid heavily on my forearm, though I'd buckled it as tight as it would go. When I was hot enough, I would take it off and leave it on a rock, and check how long it took to swim to the end of the pier and back.

That was how I got the idea to swim across the deep end of our small cove: I remember thinking that it wouldn't matter if I couldn't make it, I could always turn around and swim back in. It was warm, and the wind had just begun to come up from the southwest, darkening the water with ripples as I waded in. In a few strokes the rocks and seaweed disappeared below me into silty rays of light, and I stopped looking down and tried to concentrate on my breathing. I felt the ocean open up around me, dark and cold. Mr. Blackwell had once caught a small shark out by Hanson's Point. There was no reason to think they didn't sometimes come all the way into the bay. I tried to think about stretching my arms out in front of me and pulling them fast down the length of my body, but still I could feel myself being carried out further. I started counting strokes, keeping my sights on the channel marker I was aiming for, but it wasn't getting closer. I was rolling all the way over on my side to breathe, but the waves had begun to lurch around me as I slipped further into the bay, and I was swallowing more and more water.

I could feel the cold. It hurt at first but after a few minutes the pain started to fade, and for whole moments I felt feverishly warm. I kept swimming, trying again to count my strokes—up to five, then ten, then twenty—and as the waves got bigger and the last of my warmth left me, I started imagining I was a fish, that my body was thinning and flattening, that my mouth and salty lips gasped open and closed on a translucent hinge. Finally I just began to swim, swim toward the channel marker I could see in front of me, imagining the flash of my tail, the flash of other fish swimming beneath me, my father up high, up high on land in our dry warm house.

When I got close to the channel marker I saw that there was nowhere to hold on. The tide was pulling it violently to one side, exposing the rust below, sharp and scabrous, and a fringe of algae that heaved and swelled at its water line. I swallowed more water as I tried to breathe, kicking against the sweeping current.

Ten, twenty, forty, I counted, my arms stiffening with the cold. One, two, three, I was counting, when Mr. Blackwell's boat reared up in front of me: one, two, three.

As he pulled me out of the water I scraped against the side of the boat and landed like a fish in the bilge. *I've been caught,* I thought. My eyes stung so much with salt that I kept them closed, but I could feel the sun, and I could breathe. Mr. Blackwell said nothing when I told him I'd wanted to swim to the mainland, but he put me in an old rain slicker to cut the wind, and I felt his boat turn toward home. I pulled the coat tight around me, wishing it were as tight as my skin. The front of it was stained with fish blood.

I sat up as he turned into the cove, and he held me by the elbow and helped me out of the boat. For a moment I was afraid he would ask for the coat back—it seemed like it would tear at my flesh if I took it off.

"Put that hood over your head," he said instead, his eyes hard with worry. "That's what champion swimmers do."

I put the hood over my head and we walked up the hill toward the house. All I could see were my feet on the path; I felt my toe cut on a rock, but I kept walking, listening to the sound of my breath rasping inside the warm, musty hood.

"Is it six?" my father asked, looking vaguely over at the grandfather clock when the screen door slammed shut behind us. I could see his chair pulled tight into his desk, the pages of the book he was reading glowing under his bright lamp, the house dim around him.

"You smell like fish, my dear," he said. "Did you have a good afternoon?"

I tried to open my mouth to speak but nothing came out. I saw him put down his pen. When he stood I could see only his waist, the wrinkles of his smoothly ironed shirt tucked around his neat belt buckle. He was moving toward me, blocking the desk light.

"I found her in the channel," said Mr. Blackwell.

My father crouched down and tilted back my hood. I felt him focusing on my pale face, my blue lips—imagining his alarm pouring over me like warmth. Sometimes I still try to convince myself that the minute he saw how cold I was he took Mr. Blackwell's fishing slicker off me and wrapped me in something soft. Or that he ran a warm bath, and gave me some tea, or whiskey.

"That's a very long way," he said, straightening up, as if he didn't believe him.

"She was caught in the tide."

"We're lucky you were there to rescue her, then," my father said, with a strange smile. "Aren't we?"

Mr. Blackwell looked him straight in the eye. I thought he might hit him. He seemed suddenly to be twice my father's size, his big hands hanging like weights from his thick, brown arms. "You oughtta keep a better eye on her," he said.

"I'll keep that in mind," my father said, but Mr. Blackwell had already turned away from him.

"You take care now," Mr. Blackwell said to me, brushing his big hand gently across the top of my head.

My father just stood there. I went upstairs to bed, numb as a soldier. It seemed like hours before he came after me, though maybe it was only minutes—I had already sunk into a feverish sleep.

He pulled up my covers, though they were already at my chin. "How are you feeling?" he asked when I opened my eyes.

"Okay," I said, looking at him. "I lost your watch."

He nodded, his eyes shining in the dark.

"Did Mr. Blackwell go home?" I asked after a minute, as if I didn't know. When he didn't answer I got my arm out from under the covers and held his hand. But he took it away and asked me to come downstairs and rest on the couch. I got out of bed obediently; he put the blanket around my shoulders like a robe and brought down my pillow.

I lay on the couch and watched him sit down at his desk, but after a few minutes I stood up and went over to him. "Will you read me your book?" I asked, and when he said yes I climbed into his lap. Instead of asking me to get down he pulled me closer. I could feel his breath in my hair, his solid chest behind me.

"From the beginning," I said, though I knew it by heart. He turned the manuscript back to the first page, and then his voice rumbled through me as if it were my own:

> My purpose is to tell of bodies changed into different bodies. You heavenly powers, since you were responsible for those changes, as for all else—look favorably on my attempts, and spin an unbroken thread of verse, from the beginnings of the world, down to my own times. . . .

2

In Book One of *Metamorphoses,* Ovid tells the story of the world taking shape. Chaos is transformed into an ordered universe: a god separates sea from air, earth from heaven. The earth is rolled into a tidy ball, and water is spread over it and commanded to swell into waves at the influence of the rushing winds. Mountains peak and plains unroll; the sky is lit with stars and the sea with glittering fish. Mankind, standing erect among the beasts and rivers and flowers, ushers in the golden age. There is no law, and no threat of punishment, no city or sword; the earth goes unfurrowed and the sea unexplored.

It is in the second age, the Age of Silver, that Jove takes the reign of his father's happy kingdom, and his brother Saturn is banished to the underworld. Springtime is shortened and summer, fall, and winter follow mercilessly. Mankind seeks shelter from the cold wind and the aching heat. Jove's sister Ceres gives the gift of corn and watches mankind drive beasts to till long furrows in her fields; the stones he clears build innocent walls.

In the Age of Bronze mankind's furrows begin to deepen, his walls grow higher. Metals are soon to become weapons, and war will be the only work. But in this third age, though man is brazen, he knows his place in the newly ordered world. He is proud of the weight of his new plough—and now it is sharp—but he knows he cannot hasten the harvest, and every day the dark, freshly turned soil is a new gift. It is not until the fourth age, the Age of Iron, that man sheds his modesty for greed and lives for plunder.

In this age, the last age, the first tree is hewn, the first ship built. Man finds freedom in trickery, and as his sails fill with wind his affections scatter. Jealousy and hatred take root and flourish between lovers and friends. Iron, stolen from the bowels of the earth—and even worse, gold—fuel the fires of war. Finally the brutes covet the gods' own sanctuary, and, piling mountains one on top of another, attempt to reach the stars. Jove, watching with disgust, throws a thunderbolt through Olympus and the mountain shatters, crushing the entire foolish race. But when still another, crueler race springs from the blood-soaked earth, the gods meet in council and decide, once and for all, to flood the world.

Ovid's description of this flood takes up many verses, and my father was particularly proud of his translation of it. Though he couldn't tell, looking out our kitchen window, where the wind was coming from, he would read to me with relish of how Jove darkened the world and locked up the North Wind to let the South Wind rule. The South Wind's beard and hair were permanently dripping with rain. He spread the sea with waves and filled the air with water. When there was not water enough in heaven, Neptune summoned rivers and springs with a strike of his trident, and fed the ocean until it had no shores. Dolphins took to the woods; birds, finding no place to rest, fell into the waves. The earth, at last, was nothing but liquid: it lay before the gods like their own unending mirror.

If we were reading from the beginning, this was the end of the story. This was bedtime, lights out, and the murmur of my father and Mr. Blackwell downstairs, the clink of ice, a whiskey bottle against a glass. There are fifteen books in Ovid's poem about the transformative power of the gods from the beginning of the world to his own time. The flood is not even the end of the first. There are endless myths and fantastic legends to come, and my father read these too: passionate love stories and wonder tales of miracle and change.

It was Mr. Blackwell who finally asked what happened after the flood, and my father told us both without interest: two representatives of mankind are spared. They are in a rowboat which runs aground on the peak of Parnassus. Deucalion is the son of Prometheus, and Pyrrha is the daughter of a Titan. They are husband and wife. Later he read, with something like scorn, about how they made their way through the mud to kiss the damp marble of a half-submerged temple of Themis, its majestic columns discolored by foul moss. The oracle told them to depart from the temple, veil their heads, loosen their garments, and throw behind them "the bones of your great mother."

Deucalion and Pyrrha were horrified. How could they disturb the graves of their mothers? This riddle thrilled me. Deucalion and Pyrrha struggle at first. Pyrrha, trembling, refuses the oracle's bidding and begs her forgiveness. But Deucalion surmises that the oracle is holy and would never ask such a thing. The answer is that the oracle was speaking of the mother earth; the "bones" are stones buried in the earth's body. Once I heard this story I wanted my father to read it over and over again. I loved knowing the answer to the riddle. And I loved how they went down the hillside with veiled heads and loosened tunics, throwing stones behind them: it was like a silly game I might have played on the beach. I used to imagine them giggling, glancing fearfully at each other, afraid to look over their shoulders at the trail of dumb rocks, trying to make themselves believe in it.

The stones, needless to say, began to transform. Aside from the story of Galatea, this was one of the few metamorphoses in which human beings were the final and not the original form. They grew up behind Deucalion and Pyrrha like unfinished statues. They'd lost their previous hardness and the damp earthy parts took the form of flesh; the dry, inflexible parts became bone. In time they became women in the hands of female sculptors, and men in the hands of male sculptors.

"So we're made of rock," Mr. Blackwell responded, amused. Though I knew he loved my father's stories, he always greeted them with healthy skepticism.

"In Latin it reads: *'inde genus durum sumus experiensque laborum / et documenta damus qua simus origine nati,'*" my father answered, showing off. "'Hence come the hardness of our race and our endurance of toil; and we give proof from what origin we are sprung.'"

"Well, some of us give proof," Mr. Blackwell teased.

Mr. Blackwell had been a fisherman all his life. His mother was a Passamaquoddy Indian, but she'd worked in the sardine factories and raised him on the docks. When he was growing up sardine factories had lined the waterfront: Whistles blew all day long for incoming boats—two for fish, four for packers, five for machine operators. At the sound every woman in town picked up her apron and scissors and went to the docks for a ten-hour shift of snipping fish heads. Children came after them, packing the cans into crates.

Everyone in Yvesport but my father and I called Mr. Blackwell "Blackie." His first name was Jonas but in the summer his skin tanned to a deep red-brown and he was darker than all the other fishermen. His long, almond-shaped blue eyes got as light as the sea. Still when fishing was good there wasn't a boat in town that wouldn't take him on as crew. He had crewed on one of the first big American purse seiners, which netted huge schools of herring in open water, a method of fishing which—though none of the fishermen knew it then—turned out to be the beginning of the end of the industry. Eventually he'd made enough money to buy his own boat, the *Sylvia B.,* and hired two or three men to come out with him for weeklong seining trips in season.

He'd never been married, and I think at first it seemed natural that he'd help us out. Everyone in town, except for Mr. Blackwell, called my father "the professor"—but the joke, of course, was that he didn't know anything. Mr. Blackwell, on the other hand, knew everything. There wasn't any way to run telephone wires or electricity out to the house, and it was Mr. Blackwell who helped my parents set up a radio and a generator, and buy a small fishing boat, *Miss Suzy,* for when the weather was too rough for the dory. After my mother died he taught my father how to cook, and that spring he built a swing for me off the old oak in front of the house while he and my father fixed the roof and rebuilt the porch. When I was old enough he taught me how to skin a fish, how the tides worked, and how to steer the dory through fog as thick as milk.

It was his idea that I go to school. I was five, and my father, who was already teaching me to read, didn't see the point in my spending time with "illiterate children." Mr. Blackwell didn't argue with him: he signed me up for Yvesport Elementary and told him he was taking me. He helped me make molasses cookies for the first day, carefully counting out enough for each of the fifteen children in the class to have two. I was excited. I packed the cookies in a tin and in the morning I asked Mr. Blackwell to braid my hair tight. I held the tin close on the way over, to keep it from dropping into the cold ocean, and wouldn't let go even to hold his hand on the walk up the hill from the dock. But when I got to the classroom all I could do was hold on to his pant leg and stare.

The mothers were there with their children, holding on to the girls and scolding the boys, who were already chasing each other and knocking down chairs. I remember thinking there were too many people—I didn't have enough cookies and I wanted to go home. The teacher came over and introduced herself. She leaned down encouragingly and asked my name, a thin gold necklace with a little heart on it swinging forward between her breasts. "Do you want your father to stay a little while?" she said.

I looked up at her, my mouth shut tight, and Mr. Blackwell looked down at me and winked. I nodded. It felt like the first lie I'd ever told and I remember the excitement of it, the intimacy of having a secret, like love itself. I held his hand again and together we watched the mothers kiss their children goodbye. The children picked up toys, joined in games, and forgot their mothers before they were out the door.

"Should we give the cookies to the teacher?" Mr. Blackwell asked me.

I nodded and he waited until she'd said goodbye to all the mothers, and then he brought me over. "Miranda made some cookies for the kids," he said. "There're two for each of them."

"How nice!" she said. "Did your mother help you make them?"

I shook my head, looking at Mr. Blackwell. Were we going to lie about this too?

"Her mother's passed away," he said. "I'm just taking her in for her father. They live out on Crab Island."

"Oh," she said, looking at me with surprise. "I'm sorry."

Everyone in Yvesport knew about my mother and I can only remember a handful of times that I had had to explain it; it must have been the same for Mr. Blackwell, who took me everywhere those days.

"She's doing alright," Mr. Blackwell said warmly. "Her father's kept her busy with learning to read."

I saw her look at him like she hadn't really heard. For some reason telling people your mother is gone always makes them think of themselves. In the stories my father read me from *Metamorphoses* the mothers were the ones looking for their daughters: Ceres, goddess of the earth, searching for the missing Proserpine, stolen in the midst of gathering flowers, by Pluto, the tyrant of the underworld, and brought by his dark horses to sit beside him in his lonely palace.

There is a Sicilian water nymph, Cyane, who rises from her pool in an attempt to rescue Ceres's daughter, and when Pluto, determined to have his prize, hurls his royal scepter to the earth and breaks open the gates of his kingdom once and for all, Cyane begins to weep and cannot stop. Her limbs melt away, her dark hair, her hands, her feet—into a whirl of current, until finally she is only a spring in the pool where she was once a powerful spirit. When Ceres, continuing to search without rest for her daughter, comes back to Sicily and visits Cyane, the mournful nymph has no mouth or tongue with which to tell her where her daughter has gone. In desperation Cyane stirs her own waters until Proserpine's girdle floats to the top.

When Ceres sees the telltale garment her panicked search turns to rage: still uncertain whom to blame, she turns against her faithful earth, causing seeds to spoil and crops to perish on their first shoots—now by too much sun, now by torrential rain and storms. It takes the interference of yet another nymph to stop her destruction: Arethusa tells her she has seen her daughter in the underworld, enthroned beside the king of darkness. Ceres demands her daughter back, but Jove, who is the father, forces her to compromise: he will return the daughter to her mother for one half of the year, but the other half she must spend with her husband.

The story, of course, is meant to explain the winter and spring: when Proserpine is gone her mother is sad and the world is barren and empty; when she returns the world erupts in cheerful sunshine and new growth. When I asked my father what would have happened if Ceres had died instead, Mr. Blackwell had piped up from the kitchen: "There'd be no more farmers and everyone would be a fisherman."

"But neither would Proserpine have any reason to leave her kingdom," my father had replied, more to Mr. Blackwell than to me.

Mr. Blackwell was at the stove with his back to us. "I bet she could think of a reason," he'd said, flipping over the grilled cheese sandwich he was making for me.

I knew he was my reason, and that he was my father's too. When we were alone my father and I were in our own dark kingdom. I was quiet in the house, and if my father was not writing or reading a book, he was often staring blindly out the window. I didn't think he was thinking about my mother. We almost never spoke of her, and the few pictures we had up of her in the house had begun to look unfamiliar to me as soon as she was gone. Mr. Blackwell said she was shy, but in the pictures we had she looked distant, as if she had stepped into a fog to lose herself just before each shutter snapped.

When another winter came around and the island was covered with snow Mr. Blackwell still came over for supper, brought venison in season, leaned against the counter with a drink while my father chopped onions the way Mr. Blackwell had taught him—rocking one long knife back and forth with both hands, getting it done quick as possible, to shorten all the crying. More often than not he stayed after dinner, and he and my father took a bottle of whiskey into the living room and sat by the fire after I went to bed.

After I started going to school Mr. Blackwell went to the Peavey Library to get me the books I told him we were reading—silly rhymes and colored creatures I knew my father would disapprove of. I would not read them in front of the other children in school, but I read them for Mr. Blackwell while he cooked, and he nodded discreetly as I struggled to get to the end of each page. Once, as I was stumbling along, my father joined in from his desk in the living room, in a funny high-pitched voice.

"Who was that?" Mr. Blackwell said to me when I looked up in surprise.

"The grouch," my father answered, making a face.

All three of us burst into laughter, me in wild giggles, and for a moment I felt happiness sweep across the room like a beam from the lighthouse.

I helped them paint the porch they built together that spring, and later when Mr. Blackwell persuaded my father to help him repair the roof they let me come up the ladder as long as I sat close against the chimney. There was a chill in the air but they worked with their shirts off, my father's back and shoulders pink from the sun, his chest a frightening white. Mr. Blackwell moved as if he were on level ground, and my father strained to keep up with him, concentrating on every nail, straightening up only to wipe the sweat from his glasses. Across the water I could see the harbor, Yvesport clustered on the other side of the channel, the boats and houses and empty sardine factories leading around the point to Estes Head Pier and Deep Cove. I leaned against the chimney's warm, sooty-smelling bricks, glad that we had left the rest of the world behind.

3

If you aren't born in Yvesport, then you are "from away," no matter how young you are when you arrive. I knew that this alone would always separate my father and me from everyone else in town, much the way, despite his local heritage, Mr. Blackwell's Indian blood would always separate him. But then each of us also had our own particular way of not fitting in. My father almost never landed the boat properly when he picked me up, whether he was driving the dory or *Miss Suzy,* and when Mr. Blackwell was on a fishing trip I dreaded going down to the dock after school and waiting for my father to come in, revving the engines and swearing at the gap between the boat and the dock.

Mr. Blackwell never rushed the *Sylvia B.,* and always pulled her up to the dock to rest her there within an inch of where I was standing. If he wasn't at sea he was usually waiting for me when I got out of school, fixing something on her, or was somewhere around, leaning over another fisherman's engine well to diagnose an unfamiliar rattle or repair a slipped crank. Whomever he was working with would quietly finish up their questions as soon as they saw me, letting him go as if his shift had begun. We would get in the *Sylvia B.* together and I would untie the lines while he let the motor amble.

She cut through the water with a hefty kind of grace, and once we were out of the harbor in open water, his gaze would settle somewhere beyond her bow, and they would find their own pace, like a horse and rider might, whatever the length of the journey.

I wouldn't see inside his house on the mainland until after he and my father stopped speaking, but I had seen it from his truck on the rare occasion that he had to pick something up and brought me with him. It was a trailer on the south side, down the hill and well away from school in a cluster of other small houses and mobile homes. He had built a neat porch outside the front door and had a small yard which he kept mown in the short summer months. Beside the other houses, with their patched-up windows and piles of couches and bicycles out in front, it had an unmistakable air of propriety and privacy; it was not the sort of house that invited you inside.

The only house I visited with relative frequency in Yvesport when I was a child was Julie Peabody's. Her father owned the bank, and she might have been the only girl in my class who had enough social status to be able to afford a friendship as odd as mine.

"I have that book," she said to me one day in my second year of school, when I was inside reading during recess and everyone else was out in the playground.

"I'm just looking at the pictures," I said, closing it.

"Why don't you come outside?" she said, as if she didn't care whether I could read or not. She had her hair in two perfect, bouncy ponytails, red baubles attached to the elastics that matched the strawberries in her pretty dress. My hair was long, and I knew it was snarled and matted. Mr. Blackwell often said I ought to cut it, which I wouldn't have minded, but neither of them liked doing it themselves, and sometimes it was years before one or the other of them remembered to take me to the hair salon in town. Julie's shoes matched her dress, and I thought she must have a whole lineup of colored shoes at home. She was like a doll, and probably had a whole lineup of them too. I looked at her, not sure if I was frightened or jealous.

She looked right back at me and asked if I was from New York. When I said yes she said her mother had been there, the same way she'd told me she owned the book I was reading, but as she said it I finally saw a spark of jealousy. Once I had something to offer it was different; I went outside with her to play. From that moment on no matter what clothes I wore, or how infrequently I washed my hair, she made sure that I was the one whose hand she held when we were marched into town, that I had a desk next to hers in every class, and that we were on every team together. I never let her down. She knew how to play the games, but I was a fast runner; I could read and spell but she was the one with the neat handwriting; I knew the answers but she put her hand up.

Her house was on Favor Street, north of school. When I visited her mother would give us a glass of milk and two store-bought cookies on a plate. She had a younger brother, who liked to duck under the table. "I'm a dog!" he would say, and Julie's mother would look frightened, as if she almost believed him, until Julie gave him a kick and made him cry. Then her mother would pick him up and hold him as if he were a baby.

Julie had her own room, with an empty white bookshelf she had lined with miniature horses and a small table with chairs and a tea set. All the bedrooms in the Peabody house had printed quilts and smelled of freshly washed sheets. Her mother was always somewhere in the house, folding things, while we played. She did have dolls, which were meant to be from different countries—the red-haired girl with the kilt from Scotland, the black-haired girl with the flamenco dress from Spain—but under their dresses they were exactly the same, and each of them had the same tiny shoes with cardboard soles and the same plastic feet with scored toes. I treated them with respect, trying to find the thing about them that would convince me they were truly from faraway places, but Julie treated them with awe, and arranged them back on the shelf in the same order every time, as if they had a logic she could never defy.

When I was with Julie I always had the feeling I was too quiet and serious, but at home I was never serious enough. The alliance that had formed between my father and Mr. Blackwell was based on nothing if not their mutual seriousness. Though they seemed like opposites to most people in Yvesport—one too practical to get anything wrong, the other too preoccupied to get anything right—at heart they were both men without compromise. If my father went into town he rarely went anywhere with Mr. Blackwell, but I remember seeing them standing together once, dressed in their good clothes at Tim Ballard's funeral, and to me they seemed more serious than the priest himself.

I brought Julie over to my house only once, after I learned to drive the boat myself and just before Mr. Blackwell went back to fishing. I had forgotten my homework, which was not uncommon, but Julie wanted to copy it, and somehow she persuaded me to let her go home with me in the middle of the morning. Mr. Blackwell had shown me how to treat everything in the boat with care, and we had pored over nautical charts of the bay and all the islands, reading depth and distances in codes and tiny numbers, tracing channels and fishing territories so that I could use a compass. I always followed the exact path he drew for me, straight lines on the charts, using landmarks and buoys to guide me. But that morning with Julie I jumped into the dory and made a flashy show of starting the engine, which I managed in one pull, and told Julie casually that she didn't have to wear her life jacket.

It was late spring and the bay had the sharp sparkle it does when there is no haze. I had a quick thrill of pride at the way the house would look, hidden from view by the newly green trees, the lilacs just blooming. As we came out of the breakwater I headed straight for the channel marker until we were so close that Julie screeched. I veered off and she turned and grinned at me excitedly. I saw the *Sylvia B.* on the pier as we came around to the cove, and I remember thinking that it was odd; Mr. Blackwell was supposed to be on a trip, and if he came back early I always saw the boat at the town dock in the morning.

Julie looked eagerly up at the house as I landed. "Is your father home?" she asked.

I knew that minute that I had made a mistake. My father would not like being interrupted. And I didn't know what Mr. Blackwell was doing; I didn't see the washing on the line, or any sign of him working outside—a ladder against the house, or the wheelbarrow by the garden. As we walked up to the porch I was already thinking of excuses: the house was locked and I had forgotten the key; my father was asleep and we couldn't disturb him; I had forgotten to do the homework and it wouldn't be any good to her anyway. But my father came to open the door before we'd gotten there.

He hardly glanced at Julie; he put his finger to his lips and shut the screen door carefully behind him. "Jonas is sleeping," he whispered.

"I came to get my homework," I said, confused, not sure why he was using Mr. Blackwell's first name.

He looked at me. "Well, go and get it," he said. "I don't want you to wake him up."

I looked back at Julie, who gave me a nervous smile. I knew she didn't want to be left on the porch with my father and impulsively I beckoned her inside with me before my father could stop us. Mr. Blackwell was lying on the couch, his mouth open, snoring peacefully. He had his head on a pillow at one end, and his large naked feet on the other. One arm was curled sleepily on his chest and the other was wrapped around his waist, his hand grasping his belt.

"Was that Mr. Blackwell?" she whispered when we got to my room, as if she'd never seen him before.

"Yes," I answered, grabbing my homework from my desk.

"What's he doing?" she said. She had barely glanced around my room.

"Sleeping, I guess," I said. I had wanted her to see my neatly made bed, adorned with a quilt Mrs. Pierce had given us; I had wanted to show her the picture of my mother, which I'd never shown to anybody but Mr. Blackwell. But then there was nothing really for me to say about the picture, and she wouldn't have understood that anyway.

It did not surprise me that friendship was disappointing—I had probably disappointed her too, not looking enough at her little horses, her dolls. I turned reluctantly to go back downstairs, dreading Mr. Blackwell's sleeping, my father's ridiculous protectiveness. Loneliness descended on me like a cold fog. We passed by Mr. Blackwell's feet—long, brown, and bony—perched on the end of the couch like two still birds, and then my father opened the door for us, mindful again of the squeaky hinges.

"He hasn't slept in days," he said to me in a hushed voice.

Julie was watching him curiously. He'd hardly been in town at all since I'd learned to drive the boat—it had probably been years since she had seen him. Suddenly I wished with a kind of vengeful despair that he was someone else, and that he'd said hello to her, and combed his hair, and smiled at us both. I turned away from him and headed back down to the boat. Julie followed me, ready to get back on the water where we could bounce over the waves and she could scream like she was really scared.

4

Once the market for herring was gone Mr. Blackwell's trips got longer. Other fishermen started trawling for scallops, talking about salmon farms, and going into trucking. People in Yvesport blamed the environmentalists, who'd regulated the industry too late, or the canneries, who couldn't keep up, or the packagers, who'd let sardines go out of fashion after the war years—some people even blamed the Russians, who had come over with their radars and their milewide nets. I noticed only that Mr. Blackwell slept more when he was around, and that my father started acting less concerned, and more impatient.

The last time he had supper with us before he left me back in my father's care was the summer before my fifth-grade year. He had said he would bring some fish for us and we waited until well past sundown for him to come over with it. I was drawing at the kitchen table, and my father had already gotten out the whiskey for the night.

"Got you some lobster," he said when he finally walked in the door, bringing the bucket straight into the kitchen.

He gave me a cheerful smile, and I knew immediately that he was exhausted. My father loved lobster, but we rarely ate it because Mr. Blackwell had fished it before and seen too much of it. I knew he must not have managed to find anything else.

My father took a sip of whiskey, watching him. "I suppose you had to go swimming after each one?"

"Mark Cabbot's engine had a cylinder that needed replacing," he said unapologetically.

"We got our tests back in math today," I interrupted. I had done badly, but I wanted their attention.

My father refilled his whiskey and poured another for Mr. Blackwell, and for a minute I thought he hadn't heard me. "I've never found math very useful," he said after he'd taken a sip. "*Blackie* probably thinks it's the cornerstone of learning, however."

Mr. Blackwell looked at him. I'd never heard my father use his nickname. Without a word he walked over and picked up the drink my father had poured him. "Never liked math much myself," he said, taking a sip.

"You're being modest," my father persisted. "You were one of those boys who were good at engines, weren't you?"

Mr. Blackwell looked into his glass, deciding whether or not to respond. "Seems to me your daughter wants to tell you how she did on the test."

I kept my eyes down, unwilling to take sides.

"And fishing," my father continued, as if he was in the middle of a sentence. "Engines and fishing."

"Not sure what that has to do with math," said Mr. Blackwell.

"Nothing. Except that neither of them actually take any real *thought,* do they?" He took another sip of his whiskey. "Which is why you like them."

"You got something on your mind, Peter?" Mr. Blackwell said, putting his glass down.

"Nothing at all," my father said, giving him an ugly, fake smile. He leaned back and opened his arms wide. "Nothing on my mind at all. Utterly blank. A blank slate."

Mr. Blackwell stood up with a sigh. "How should we cook up these lobsters?" he said, picking up the bucket with one hand and walking into the kitchen.

"A fascinating question, cooking those lobsters," my father said, leaning heavily on the table. "What's for dinner? What's for breakfast? We might as well start planning now. Maybe Miranda wants to make a pie!"

Mr. Blackwell bent over the cupboard to find the big cooking pot, crashing around and noisily stacking the smaller ones on the floor beside him.

"It's above the sink," I said.

My father looked up at me as if he'd just noticed that I was in the room. Mr. Blackwell was still leaning over, hunting. "She says it's above the sink," my father shouted suddenly, at the top of his lungs.

I held my breath as Mr. Blackwell straightened up. My father looked surprised, and even frightened, as if he hadn't expected to be shouting either.

Mr. Blackwell couldn't look at him. "Thank you, Miranda," he said, giving me a small pained smile before he reached up to retrieve the pot.

My father was quiet after that, though not too ashamed to pour himself another whiskey while Mr. Blackwell and I made dinner. The lobsters boiled quickly; we cooked the whole batch. Mr. Blackwell set two aside for my father and me to eat and I brought them to the table with a baked potato and a dish of butter, the way my father liked it. Mr. Blackwell cracked the tails off the rest, removing the meat with one quick slice of his knife, smashed open the claws, and dropped in some mayonnaise for a salad, a pile of which he put on his own plate. My father tucked his napkin into his collar, and plucked off one of the skinny legs to chew on. The whiskey was slowing him down. I went at the tail of mine without much appetite. Mr. Blackwell finished off his meal in a matter of minutes and got up to wash the dishes.

We always had a rule about not getting up from the table until everyone was done eating, but for once my father didn't say a word. He was pretending to be intent upon the last of the meat in his lobster's right claw. I was trying not to watch him, but I had never seen him that drunk. Mr. Blackwell, on the other hand, had probably seen my father drunk before, but not when he himself was sober. He cleaned the pots at lightning speed, wiped down the counter, and put the rest of the salad he had made in the refrigerator. I saw him glance at my father, as if he was about to say something—apologize, maybe for being late. But then he pulled his coat on.

"I'll see you around," he said to me before he left.

I nodded, trying not to look desperate. He must have known what would happen, that eventually my father would fall asleep in his chair, but at that point I didn't know what to expect. I braced myself for more surprises—it seemed possible that my father might start shouting again, this time at me, or that Mr. Blackwell might even return, and shout back. The engine of the *Sylvia B.* roared to a start, and as Mr. Blackwell drove out of the cove, my father started back in on his lobster. In the silence I had the strange feeling that I was dreaming, and that nothing unusual had happened at all. If only I could keep eating, I told myself, the evening would continue quietly forward, and we'd wish each other good night, and in the morning I'd turn over in my bed and see the cove glittering with new daylight, and I would eat my breakfast like Julie did, and go to school like every other girl. But Mr. Blackwell had left, and I wasn't hungry.

I stood up and cleared my plate. "I'm going to bed," I said, like a command.

That night as I lay in bed waiting for the sound of my father coming up the stairs, I thought about what it would be like to see the island from far away, from high up, the way it looked on the charts and maps, the cove and the long arm of the point protect-ing the harbor. In *Metamorphoses* the gods were always soaring from one place to another, spying on nymphs from above; I felt them looking down at us, at Mr. Blackwell landing at the dock, at my father in the kitchen. But I knew they were in search of other things. They passed over the tiny boat, the harbor, the house, and the island—on their way somewhere else, somewhere busy, full of noise, alighting, turning their backs on the three of us, living on the island and refusing to change.

That was the summer I tried to swim across the cove. After Mr. Blackwell rescued me, I didn't see him until September, when he told me he'd sold the *Sylvia B.* and gotten a job at the boatyard. I was tying up our boat up at the dock on my way to school and he walked over with a paper bag in his hand and asked me if I wanted a cup of coffee.

He knew perfectly well that my father wouldn't allow me to drink coffee. He'd always kept a pot on our kitchen stove and though my father occasionally had a cup he had never let me near it. I looked up at him and for a minute I considered refusing. But I was afraid he might go away. When I said yes we walked up to a bench in the sun and he opened the bag. There were two cups of coffee and two cinnamon rolls from Suzanne's bakery inside. He took the lid off my coffee and passed it to me, and put the two cinnamon rolls down on the bag between us. I took a sip of the coffee, which was horrible, burnt acid and black, but I tried to smile, as if I liked it.

"That's a girl," he said, laughing. "Try the roll."

The roll was sweet, and wound around and around, each layer softer and more dusky with cinnamon filled with hidden raisins, until I got to the virgin-white core, baked through and buttery. I took little sips of coffee in between. I didn't tell Mr. Blackwell how quiet it was in the house, or how I'd made a custard pie on my own, or that my father had stopped drinking, and that every night at about the time when Mr. Blackwell used to come over and they'd have a drink and make dinner, my father would look up into the air from whatever he was doing, as if he was listening for some faraway signal.

Instead we simply sat beside each other in the sun and ate our rolls and drank our coffee. Since the first day of school when the teacher thought he was my father, we'd known how to keep a secret between us. If the gods had left us behind then maybe we had left them too—whatever we had, I thought, was not for them to touch.

5

In the end I didn't mind having my father to myself. Often I stayed up with him until he went to bed. He wasn't interested in helping me with my homework, and I drew at the kitchen table while he read and wrote. He was making progress on his manuscript; at some point he ordered a typewriter to be delivered to the general store, and I learned to use it. Previously I had been taking his manuscript pages to Mrs. Lynch, one of the secretaries in the school office, who would type them and give them back in a crisp manila envelope. She had a pair of eyeglasses on a thin chain around her neck and would put them on whenever she saw me coming. I often imagined turning those envelopes upside down to pour the pages into the sea as I drove home, the powdery smell of Mrs. Lynch wafting out of the envelope before the pages dropped onto the waves and sifted slowly to the bottom.

I was more than happy to learn to type. We made up a game in which my father would dictate and I would wear a blindfold, and I would lose a point for every letter I missed. Sometimes I would pretend to be making a mistake and type in the wrong word just to make him laugh. When it was his turn he could hardly get any words at all. I mentioned to Mr. Blackwell that I was learning to type and he said it was a shame my father couldn't learn to type himself.

When the channel froze just before Christmas, my father and I settled in for a few months without the mainland. The *Sylvia B.* was heavy enough to break ice almost all year round, but our own boat couldn't get through it without damage.

We had plenty of firewood and smoked fish, and we made cookies, and pots of tea, and some days he dictated and I typed. One afternoon we went out on the ice, and walked as far as the red channel marker. Its surface was rusted and rough and snagged on our wool mittens. On the way back I could tell my father was scared, and I sprinted in front of him and slid as far as I could, balancing with my arms wide. He smiled, watching me, and I stood there and waited for him to catch up. Snow flurries rushed between us, two black shapes without the world.

"We ought to keep separate on the ice," he said when he got close enough.

It was Mr. Blackwell, I found out later, who sent over the Coast Guard. There must have been other children at Yvesport who didn't go to school because of the weather that year, but I doubt the school authorities sought them out.

The morning they came was beautiful, bright, and cold. I was drawing a picture of some dry sea heather, copying the way the branches split into the air, and I saw them coming from the mainland, breaking the ice. The boat had an extra fixture on the bow, and in the cold you could see the smoke as the engine revved before the hull heaved onto the ice like a fat seal, then sank back down on the water. They took almost three hours to go the distance I would have sped across in minutes on a calm day. I didn't tell my father they were coming. I told myself I wasn't sure if they were headed for us, but in the end there was no mistaking the dark trail straight to the island. Chief Nichols, the head of the police department, led them all up the hill.

When I opened the door they all took off their hats, even though it was freezing. I wondered if they had been told ahead of time to do that, or if those were policemen's rules. A fisherman would have kept his on. "Wanted to be sure you and your dad were alright," Chief Nichols said to me.

I heard my father, pushing his chair back. All the men shifted their feet and coughed, white clouds of breath tearing away from their faces.

"What's this?" my father said, from behind me, his eyes landing on the chief.

"Morning, Mr. Donnal. Haven't seen Miranda coming across for school and we wanted to make sure you were alright," Chief Nichols said, polite.

"Well, we haven't really got the weather for crossing, have we?" my father answered, cheerfully enough. I saw his eyes flickering down to the beach, the boat on the shore. He was wearing his slippers, and his hair was standing on end; he'd been pulling at it all morning.

"Think we could come inside?" said the chief.

"Doubt I have too much choice," my father replied, smiling again, standing back and gesturing for me to do the same.

I recognized one of them, Dan MacPherson's brother John, whom Julie had once said she wanted to marry, just because he was going to the Coast Guard Academy. It occurred to me that my father had never met anyone like John MacPherson, though Mr. Blackwell would have known him—Mr. Blackwell would have known them all.

My father remained by the door, leaving it open; he looked smaller with so many men in the house, and I wished someone would sit down. Their big boots tracked in puddles of sandy snow. I busied myself putting a kettle on, as if we were all about to have tea.

The chief took off his gloves. "Don't mean to disturb you, Mr. Donnal," he said, tucking the gloves carefully into his hat as if he were building a nest, "but the school board feels that you're putting Miranda's education at risk."

"The school board?" my father repeated.

"Miranda's missed several months of school."

My father looked at him. "My daughter has been helping me to translate Ovid's *Metamorphoses*," he said.

The chief glanced down at his hat. The open door was against everyone's instincts. The other men were watching him. "Well, we went ahead and cleared a path for you, Mr. Donnal," he said, "so Miranda'll be able to come over in the morning."

"I'm certain my daughter will do whatever she likes," my father replied, his eyes twinkling, as if we'd won.

They all looked toward me and I felt my stomach turning. A pimple had broken out at the corner of my mouth that morning and I bit my lower lip, as if I could cover it up. Even the Coast Guard men knew I had never made a decision in my life.

Chief Nichols gave me a nod. As they all walked out I had the curious feeling that I should want to marry them too. They could rescue me, I thought, as they put their hats back on. I should rush after them, I thought, as I watched them walk in a soldierly line down to the beach. The kettle whistled and my father and I both rushed to turn it off.

That night I made a pie with a jar of blueberry preserves, the way I did when we finished a lengthy section. But we could hardly eat it.

"I think you need a new sweater," I said finally, when we were cleaning up, pointing out how the hem of his was unraveling.

"Perhaps I do," he said, glancing down at it.

"I'll get you one," I said, and he nodded gratefully: Both of us knew he was giving me permission to go to school in the morning. The next morning I went into the shed before the sun was up and rummaged around for fresh spark plugs, drained the treated fuel, and remounted the engine. With my father's help the boat slid easily down the frozen sand into the water. The whole bay had already begun to break apart into big fatty chunks.

Mr. Blackwell came down to the dock to meet me, holding his coffee in both hands like a candle. For a minute I was angry, but more for my father's sake than for my own. I tied up the boat without saying anything.

"I'm getting my father a new sweater today," I said, when it seemed like he was just going to let me go.

"That'll be a nice present," he said.

He didn't ask me to have coffee, though. Nobody at school asked me where I'd been either. Julie said it didn't make that much difference, with Christmas in between, but she and Donna

Morrissey were wearing the same eyeliner, and at the end of the day they left together, striding off in the direction of the gym. I picked out a red wool sweater for my father at Friedlander's, and the saleswoman wrapped it in tissue and put it in a box that was too big for my knapsack.

On the way out of the harbor it got splashed, and I was going to move it closer, but I was concentrating on the ice, and I let it fall instead into the bilge. The box opened and the sweater fell out, still folded in its tissue paper. I didn't stop the boat. When I got into the channel where the broken path had widened with the tide I turned to drive past the red channel marker and into the bay.

Before the bay froze I'd tried to tell Julie the story of Phaethon, who asked to drive his father's chariot because someone at school had asked for proof that he was the son of the sun god. He went all the way to his father's palace to get permission, and he could have asked for anything, but he wanted to drive the chariot, pulled across the sky by a team of fiery winged horses that only his father could control.

"Why did he ask for that?" Julie had said, disdainful.

"Boys like to drive things," I'd answered with a shrug, and she'd laughed.

"You like to drive things too," she'd said.

When I got into the bay I kept going, straight out. The wind cut at my face. There were still big patches of ice to avoid, but they were easy to spot; I didn't know where I was going, but I wasn't scared. Phaethon had gotten what he wanted, and despite his father's protests he'd taken the reins of the chariot and rode into the sky. The horses had panicked at his unfamiliar weight and gone wild—he'd scorched the earth, and eventually Jove had had to throw one of his lightning bolts straight into the burning mess to prevent any more damage.

I slowed the boat and cut the engine. All around me the ice flowed silently out of the bay. The water was dark and viscous, the afternoon sun hard and flat.

"I would have asked for something gold from the palace," Julie had said, fiddling dreamily with the bracelet she always wore, "so I could take it home and show everybody."

"But how would they know it was from a god?" I'd asked.

"They could just tell. It would have jewels."

"He wanted to prove it, though," I'd pushed.

She'd looked annoyed. "What would you ask for then?"

I didn't know, of course. In the stories I typed for my father everyone was always making mistakes; there was no easy answer. Nothing Phaethon could have asked for would have satisfied him. In Ovid greed and pride and lust were as inevitable as mortality.

In the weeks before the bay froze my father and I had had a kind of rhythm—I was spelling words before he said them, and pausing only when he breathed. There was a luxurious absence in my head, the way I felt when I was drawing, or just imagining things, picturing the horses, the chariot flailing across the sky. I looked out at the bay, knowing I should turn on the engine and go home. The cold had seeped into my clothes and begun to settle in me. The boat had begun to pull with the current. Finally I leaned forward and picked up his sweater, put it back in the box.

The wool was machine knit and smooth, and I brushed off the water it had touched in the bilge and folded it back into the box. I knew we wouldn't get our rhythm back. I would go home and make supper, and in the morning I'd go back to school, as if it was nothing to leave him behind, when it had seemed at last that we had gotten used to being alone together.

6

By the summer before ninth grade I never went into town unless I was going to school or shopping for supplies. On the days my father came with me, if Mr. Blackwell was on the dock, my father simply walked right past him. The first time it happened Mr. Blackwell seemed startled, but the next time his eyes were flint.

When school started Julie had become best friends with Donna Morrissey, and the two of them were going to all the basketball games. Shead High School was in the Maine Boys Basketball Championship. Sometimes I went with them. After the games everybody went to the parking lot where they stood around and smoked cigarettes. Julie usually invited me to come along but she always seemed relieved when I mumbled something about going home to cook supper, or getting back before dark. She and Donna had bought bras together, on one of their shopping trips in Bangor; she had showed hers to me in the bathroom.

Occasionally I would see Mrs. Peabody, and she would ask after my father. One day that spring she caught us in town and somehow, before we knew it, we had agreed to go on a family day trip out to Wolf Island. The Peabodys had a big white motorboat moored in Deep Cove. My father said we could cancel if it was bad weather, but the day we had arranged to meet them was bright as summer.

Julie gave me a lukewarm greeting as we got into the boat—to signify that it was my fault she was spending Saturday with her family. I had worn jeans, the way I did when Mr. Blackwell used to let me go fishing with him, and my father had worn his trusted foul-weather gear, but Julie and her mother were in shorts as if they were going for a cruise. Mrs. Peabody rushed over to kiss my father on the cheek, and my father, stiff and confused, kissed her again on the other cheek in the French manner, which she attempted, flushing, to reciprocate, just as my father backed away, nearly falling out of the boat. Everyone was relieved when Mr. Peabody shook my father's hand and showed him his fishing gear.

Julie's brother cast us off us from the mooring. He was excited, as if it was a treat for him to see his father, and as Mr. Peabody started the motor they shouted various commands back and forth. My father sat carefully in one of the swiveling plastic chairs, looking back at our wake as we left the harbor and Mr. Peabody accelerated up to full speed. Mr. Peabody shouted a few things to him and he turned his chair and pulled a smile onto his face.

Julie asked me to put sun lotion on her, and then lay down beside me on the deck, the skin on her arms and legs goose-pimpling in the breeze as we sped into the bay. I sat beside her in my jeans, holding my knees. My father was giving me less to type, but I kept the stories in my head for longer and retold them to myself when I was sitting in the back of class, or going back and forth to school. I looked out at the bay past Julie's shining legs and thought of Salmacis and Hermaphroditus.

Salmacis was a nymph, but unlike all the other nymphs who roamed hunting through the woods and streams, she was "the only naiad unknown to the fleet-footed Diana," because she would not pick up a bow, and preferred instead to "bathe her lovely limbs" in her favorite pool, comb her hair, and study her reflection. Hermaphroditus, named after his father, Hermes, messenger of the gods, and his mother, Aphrodite, the goddess of love, was a young deity who had inherited both his mother's physical passion and his father's restless sense of adventure. He loved the world as if it were his mistress, doting on the tiniest blooming woodland flower every bit as much as the highest temple spire.

When Hermaphroditus comes upon Salmacis's favorite pool he is so struck by its beauty that he fails to notice Salmacis, lingering as usual by her reflection. The minute she looks up, she falls in love with him. She pauses to primp—fixing her watery hair, adjusting her flowing garment—and then she approaches him to ask for a kiss. Hermaphroditus is terrified. He has been admiring other things. He tells her he is leaving but she persuades him to stay, telling him she'll go instead, and then she hides behind a bush and waits for another chance at him.

Julie got up to go get something warmer, and I closed my eyes, imagining Salmacis turning back to the pool as soon as he thinks she is gone. The pool is quiet, and it doesn't take long before he is stepping from one rock to another, noticing the way the sunlight dips in through the clear water to magnify the pebbles on the bottom. When he strips off his clothing and walks in, the cool water tickles his calves, then his thighs, before he dives. "I have won! He is mine!" Salmacis cries as soon as she sees the splash, diving in after him, like the hunter she is supposed to be. Hermaphroditus feels her latching on. He struggles to free himself, but she wraps her legs around him and won't let go. He can't pry her off—she pulls at him, needy as a whirlpool. He feels he might drown. He twists in confusion, trying to find her—trying to find her mouth. He kisses her to appease her. Her hands hunt all over his back, she presses against him in the water, and he presses into her, but still she cries out for the gods to make them closer. The gods answer: their bodies begin to condense, her soft breasts melting into his hard chest, their legs twining together, until Hermaphroditus cries out, surrendering, and they are one body, neither a woman nor a man.

"You okay?" Julie asked, handing me her glass of lemonade and sitting back down beside me. She had a blanket wrapped around her, and her hair was streaming back in the wind. I took a sip and passed the lemonade back when she was settled.

We could see our destination already, a small cove like the one in front of our house, and we tied the boat to a stump on shore. Julie's mother got lunch out of the cooler, still packing and unpacking things. Mr. Peabody offered my father a beer and when he declined all they had was lemonade, which I knew would be too sweet for him. I also knew he didn't like eating in the sun, and I watched nervously as he accepted his ham sandwich, which I was sure he didn't like either. Julie was telling me how she was on a diet and wouldn't have any brownies, when I heard Mrs. Peabody say brightly, "You and Miranda ought to get out more, Peter."

I looked over at him and saw the spark of impatience in his eyes that he'd had ever since he quit drinking. "Is that right?" he said to her.

"We all wonder what you're doing over there, all by yourselves."

"I'm sure you do, Alice," he said with a condescending smile, "but it can't be nearly as exciting as what you imagine."

She laughed uncertainly, avoiding his eye, and then took a sip of lemonade. "Well, we do like going out in the boat," she said, looking around the shores of the cove with false contentment. "But I guess you two are out on the ocean all the time."

"Not if I can avoid it."

He hadn't meant to hurt her feelings I don't think, but he'd said it sharply, and she blushed.

"He gets seasick," I interceded from across the cockpit.

My father took a sip of the lemonade and winced, and Mrs. Peabody got up quickly to put things back into the cooler. I felt for a minute like I hated her, and Julie too. All of them.

On the way back Julie went up into the bow and I stayed beside my father. I put my hand out over the side to feel the cold coming up from the water. Mr. Blackwell had once described for me the way that molecules of cold air rising up from the bay combined with molecules of hot air rolling off the land and formed the thick banks of fog the island was shrouded in every morning and evening. I'd always wondered, though, about the place where the two met: whether it was the cold that surrendered to warm, or the air that surrendered to the water. It seemed to me there must have been a place, a moment of pause, before they were either.

I put my hand on my father's knee. He was staring out at our wake again, watching the island recede, and I knew he wished we were already home.

"We'll be home soon," I said close to his ear.

He looked at me with surprise, as if that wasn't what he was thinking at all.

7

He started drinking again a few months after that, one night when I'd made nothing but navy bean soup. We had fresh bread to go with it, but for years I wondered if he would have had that glass of whiskey if I'd served a better supper. He'd poured it just before he sat down, in one of the heavy whiskey glasses he always got out for Mr. Blackwell. It seemed to have gotten there on its own, the bronze light of the liquor half filling the glass, like an unanticipated guest. We were both mindful of it, almost polite, and when he finally took a sip, it was without ceremony, as if that way I might not notice. He closed his eyes, just briefly, and when he opened them again he was the same.

I don't know what kind of change I was expecting. I went to school every day and he went slower on the manuscript, and on the rare afternoons he had something for me to type I could finish it in a few minutes. Sometimes he would put a hand on the back of my chair, lean over to see how far I had gotten, and I would shiver at the smell of liquor on his breath. But other times I would wander over to him, ask the spelling of a word I couldn't make out, and when he pulled me in close to frown at whatever page I held he was nothing but himself, concentrating.

Shead basketball team got into the championship again se-nior year, and without Julie to keep me company I got in the habit of drawing between classes and then during classes. Mostly I drew flowers, filling the margins of my textbooks with patterns of ivy and blossoms. The only plant I could really draw without actually looking at it was a tree. I drew them with and without leaves; I drew them with knots in their trunks and crags in their branches and with roots cutting across the mossy ground. When summer came around again I started taking a thermos of coffee with me to go out and sketch wildflowers before my father woke up. That July when the meadow on the south side of the island flooded with purple towers of lupine I spent nearly a week there, trying to translate the purple and blue into black and white. Some of the stalks were dark to the tip, and others were faint, almost white at the top, and bloomed fat and velvety in the middle. I drew one stalk after another, the splay of leaves at the bottom, the pairs of ascending petals, cupping themselves, the pods before they broke, the burnt look they got when they began to die. In the night when I had trouble sleeping I went down to the living room and drew my hands: open palms, fists, lone fin-gers. My father said it was all the coffee, but I felt restless in a way I hadn't before.

One night when I was drawing he came into the kitchen and stood squinting at me in the bright lamplight. "Haven't you had that nightgown an awfully long time?" he said.

"I guess so," I said, pulling my feet under it, though I wasn't cold. In fact I'd had it nearly ten years; the hem, which had once touched the floor, was almost as high as my knees. It was one of the softest things I owned. I'd had to rip open the collar to make it bigger, so it wouldn't strangle me when I twisted around in the middle of the night, and the arms hung open at the elbows. I lifted the sketch pad to my chest and I saw his eyes drop quickly to the floor.

"Julie's always saying I should go clothes shopping," I said.

"Well, you ought to, then," he said abruptly, turning away.

I looked after him, watching his slippers go up the stairs, and then back at the hand I had begun to draw, nothing now but a meaningless shaded line. When had I grown too big for my nightgown? I went to the bathroom to look at myself in the mirror. My long legs stuck out of the bottom of my nightgown like an oversize doll's, my breasts showed beneath the tear at the neck.

At the end of the summer I decided to visit Mr. Blackwell and show him the drawings I'd done. I left the dory at the dock and went down the road to his neat house. His curtains were drawn, and all I could see from the road was the position of the dishwashing soap, like the silhouette of a woman, behind the kitchen curtains. The house next door had a mattress leaning against the side of it, and I thought about how he would have preferred that they took it away. He had lined his small wooden porch with flower boxes, full of pink and blue primrose, totally unlike the tall lilies he'd planted in front of our porch.

I knocked, but his truck was gone, and it was obvious he was still at work. I stood there, not sure what I was going to say to him anyway. The flowers and strange shadowy hands and fists inside my sketchbook were not the sort of thing we'd ever talked about. He'd know all the flowers, of course, the Indian names and the English ones; he'd even know my hands. He probably knew how tall I'd grown, and even that my father had been drinking again, and that I'd gone ahead making him supper as if nothing had happened. I turned away, ashamed. Maybe he didn't want to see things like my drawings. It would probably bother him anyway that I'd been staring at things so long.

Julie and Donna were applying to college, and I'd told them as soon as the year began that I wasn't going to. Julie's father gave them his car to drive to Bangor twice a week for a course to improve their scores on the admissions tests. I knew Mr. Blackwell would have wanted me to apply, and might have kept track of things like tests, but my father didn't know about them and it was easy enough for me not to bring him the mail from school.

A few weeks into the year a boy from our class, Eric Holmes, had a party and Julie and Donna insisted I go. We all went over to Julie's house the afternoon of the party and they cut my hair up to my shoulders and dressed me up in one of Julie's dresses. Julie drove us over there and I was giddy with my new hair and my strange outfit, and happy to be included. For the first few hours neither of them seemed to mind my following them around, but soon they both disappeared purposely into the shadowy light of the bonfire, where Ted, the older boy Julie was dating, was passing around a joint. Eric Holmes appeared by my side and asked me if I was feeling alright. We ended up walking out onto the pier together, and he told me my hair looked pretty. He said he could see me going across the channel every morning from his house. Finally he kissed me, and I kissed him back.

I didn't mind it, and was just beginning to get used to his

tongue when he leaned back and asked me softly what it was like not having a mother, as if he were asking to undo my bra.

"I don't know," I said, confused. "What's it like not being a girl?"

"No, really," he said, laughing.

I looked at him. "I have a father," I said.

"I'm just asking," he said, trying to get his soft voice back.

I moved to go. He looked disappointed, but I saw him glance over at the beach, where a few people had begun to cluster around the bonfire, before he asked me where I was going. I heard Julie laugh, saw her profile in the firelight as someone offered her the joint. I left him there and walked back toward the house.

Rebecca Hemmings was crying on the porch. She peered at me, her makeup streaked down her face, hardly recognizable. She'd done something to her hair; it hung around her face in strange separated curls. I sat down beside her, thinking how ridiculous we both looked, hoping to be transformed by the one social event we had decided not to resist.

"What are you doing?" she sniffed.

"I don't know." I pulled the dress Julie had given me over my knees. "I wish I'd never come."

"Why don't you go home?" Rebecca dabbed at her eyes with the bottom of her skirt.

"I was going to wait for Julie." I looked down at the beach, sighing, but feeling braver next to Rebecca's despair. "But maybe I'll walk."

"I should go with you," Rebecca said, as if she were punishing herself.

A wave of laughter rose from the crowded bonfire. No one was left inside the house, and the music blared across the lawn toward the dark bay.

Rebecca stood up. "Let's go," she said.

Her skirt, I noticed as we headed for the driveway, had ruffles on the bottom, and they matched the ruffles at her shoulders— the whole outfit was pale blue, almost white. She was walking as if she was tired of wearing it.

"You look nice," I said.

"Thanks." She stopped when we got to the paved road to take off her sandals, and in bare feet her stride matched mine. She'd been on the track team; I'd seen her once in a uniform after school, getting picked up by her mother.

"I saw your drawing," she said, "that they put up in the library."

I felt her eyes on me. We got out of the way of a car that came from the party, and the headlights blazed on her skirt. Someone hollered something out the window at us as the car screeched down the road.

"Are you applying to college?" she asked.

"No," I said, watching the taillights wink out down the road. The darkness pressed on my skin in a comforting way. I could still hear the noise of the party behind us, but the trees lining the road were dark and indifferent. Great Neck was where the summer people lived, and the houses twinkled at the ends of their long driveways, nearly out of sight.

"I want to go to MIT," she said when I didn't ask. She swung her sandals wide, as if she was cheering herself up. "Julie's applying, right?"

"Yeah," I said, remembering now how Rebecca had been good at math, better than most of the boys.

Suddenly she stopped and grabbed my arm. "What's that?" she whispered.

Her hand felt warm, almost hot, against my cool skin; she kept it there, holding tight. "A fox," I said. It stopped, perfectly still, to look at the two of us, its ears perked up high, its eyes glistening. The white of its chest flashed as it started for the woods with an easy skulk, leaving us, standing as still as it had been, to watch it go.

"Is it dangerous?" Rebecca asked.

"No," I said, as she let go of my arm, wondering what she would have done if I'd said yes. But then the fox had seemed so dignified, so coolly indifferent—she would have known, I thought, that I was lying. Her skirt glowed in the dark and I watched it moving as she walked, her broad feet now unsure on the pavement. It seemed like she was staying closer; it was exciting, this feeling that I knew more than she did. I felt glad for all the foxes out there hunting, and found myself hoping that another one might skulk across our path. At one point an owl hooted loudly from the woods and I looked at Rebecca expectantly, but she didn't notice; she sniffed again and I remembered how she had been crying before.

"Were you kissing Eric Holmes on the dock?" she asked.

"No," I lied.

She kept her eyes straight ahead. I'd known I was going to kiss him as soon as we'd walked toward the pier; there wasn't much else to do.

"It's okay if you were," Rebecca said, her eyes liquidy, tucking one of her strange curls behind her ear. "He kissed Julie last weekend."

"Julie Peabody?" My voice sounded loud and sharp.

Rebecca tucked the curl behind her ear again. "I bet she never told Ted."

Eric Holmes? I thought indignantly. He wasn't even handsome. "Are you sure?" I said.

Rebecca nodded, staring gloomily. I was beginning to feel foolish for having suggested that we walk; we were still miles from town, and it would probably be light by the time we got there.

"Maybe we should try to get a ride," I said, "from the next car that goes by."

"Okay," she said.

I looked over at her. "Do you think I should apply to college?"

"I don't know," she said, surprised. "My dad said he'd pay for it if they don't give me a big enough scholarship. My brother probably won't go, though. He hates school."

"So do I," I said.

She looked at me. "Why?"

I shrugged. "I like being alone," I said, though I had managed to be alone plenty in school. In fact I didn't like school because it was difficult; I wasn't good at it, though my father thought I was better than everybody else. I didn't like to study for tests, and I never did well at math. I knew I'd do terribly on the college admissions test, and he would only be disappointed.

"Are there any bears out here?" she finally said.

"Not any who would be interested in us," I answered. I heard another owl. "That's an owl," I said.

"I know *that*." She glanced at me and I caught a hint of a smile.

I took a deep breath. I could smell the sun that had been lying in the woods all day, drifting up through the cool air. It hadn't been that exciting, pressing my lips against Eric Holmes's, but I was glad I'd done it. Rebecca Hemmings was quiet. I wanted to reach out and touch her arm like she had touched mine, but I was one step away. I moved to catch up and a pair of headlights struck us from down the road.

Julie stopped her mother's station wagon beside us and put her head out the window like a train conductor. "You guys need a ride?" she yelled drunkenly.

"Who is it?" I heard Donna asking from the back. Rebecca had stopped in the shadows, just behind me. I could see Eric Holmes in the passenger seat shoving at the boy next to him.

"Quit it," Julie said to him, giggling.

Rebecca stood rigidly, one arm at her side, the other across her chest, and stared at Eric through the window. She had wiped away the streaks of mascara on her cheeks, but the black around her eyes and her strange hairdo made her look spooked.

"Do you want to go?" I asked her.

She tore her eyes away from the car just long enough to give me an impatient look, as if my hesitation might have already lost us the offer.

"You coming?" Julie said, turning her attention back to me.

"Rebecca is," I said.

"Get in front!" the boy sitting next to Eric Holmes yelled.

Rebecca started around the front of the car without even looking back at me, her eyes shining, one arm still awkwardly pressed to her side.

"We can fit you both," Julie said, distracted, as someone squealed in the back.

"That's okay," I said. "It's nice out here." I leaned down to wave at Rebecca, sliding in next to the two boys. "See you," I said. But Rebecca was busy with her skirt and the door.

"See you," Julie said merrily.

A few other cars honked as they went by, after she drove off, and I gave them a hearty wave so they could see that I was enjoying myself. I already felt my new sandals giving me blisters; I took them off and tried to go a little faster. There was almost no moon, but the sky had lightened a little between the trees above the road. I heard another owl, and hooted back in response, the way Mr. Blackwell had once taught me, but there was no answer. "That's an owl," I pictured myself saying, and shame filled me doubly, so that suddenly I had the urge to run. I didn't stop until I got to the edge of town, where there was a path down through the woods to the dock, and I could go back to pretending my father was waiting up for me at home.

8

The day of the college admissions test it was raining, and I put on my boots and foul-weather gear and drove across the water to take the bus from school. The dock was practically empty—it was late in the season for fishing, and the few boats that were there were gloomy and still. I walked up onto the road with my hood on, watching my rubber boots on the pavement, and then instead of going directly up the hill toward school I took a path through the woods. It was muddy but I thought I might see a deer; I had seen a doe on my way through a few days before. The trunks of the trees were wet, the thick roots uneven under my feet. The rain let up as I was walking, and I stopped and looked around. I stood there listening to the heavy drops left over, falling one by one from where they had collected in the leaves. I stayed perfectly still. Sometimes I could hear only the drops and sometimes I could hear a car on the road and I would think it was the bus going by. I would try not to listen.

When at last I made my way back out I knew the bus was

gone. Things in the town were more awake, I heard other cars. I went across the road and made my way down along the shore, where it was still too foggy to see more than a few feet out into the water. I wasn't walking toward McMann's and hadn't meant to go there, but it was low tide, and I came around the point before I knew it, stepping from rock to rock and coming around through the brush where I needed to, until I saw it, suspended out over the pier.

McMann's was too far out on the road between Yvesport and Pleasant Point for anyone from town to go there much. It didn't have food, but I'd heard it was busy year-round with the truckers who drove in from Canada and the sailors and crews from the container ships. When I opened the door I was too afraid to look around; I went straight in and took a stool at the bar, hanging my jacket over the stool beside me. Two old men with beers were hunched at the other end of the bar, watching a game show on television. The bartender, a woman, was watching with them, and she turned around and came reluctantly toward me.

"Coffee?" she said. She wasn't much older than I, but she seemed to feel she was. I felt conscious suddenly of the thick wool cardigan I had worn for the test, my big rubber boots over my jeans. I wished at least I had taken my hair out of the braid it had been glued into by the rain.

I cleared my throat. "Do you have any whiskey?" I asked, unable to make my voice sound anything but polite.

She glanced up at me, and for an instant I thought she might refuse, but she turned away to reach for a glass. "On the rocks?" she said coolly.

She put a few cubes in the glass with her bare hand and poured the whiskey on top. She had a tattoo on one arm—a heart with something in it—that showed beneath her shirt sleeve. "Four dollars," she said without a smile when she put the drink in front of me. She was wearing dark eyeliner, which made her face look even skinnier than it was. Her hair was black and pulled into a stringy ponytail. She had two silver hoops in one of her ears, and her T-shirt was tucked into a wide belt with a large silver buckle studded with turquoise—the kind they sold at the Wampanoag Trading Post, where they had the stuffed moose.

She went back to watching the television and I took a sip of my drink. It gave me a strange warm shiver. I recognized one of the old men, Bobby Newlin, whose wife had died three winters ago. They were watching a game show on television, where the contestants tried to spell a phrase on a big board. I got it when they put the R's up with the E's: ALTERNATIVE ROUTES. I tried to think when I'd gotten so afraid of tests; when I'd first started school they had been easy, and I'd thought my father was right that I was better at them than the other kids. I took a bigger sip of my drink, felt my stomach turn and then settle.

Bobby Newlin left and the man who stayed behind ordered a beer. The bartender gave it to him and then went over to the pool table to have a cigarette, pacing a little. I couldn't tell if she was bored or anxious. It was strange I'd never seen her before. I would have remembered her, I thought—she was the kind of girl who didn't make friends easily. She was pretty in a fierce sort of way, like she was angry. I wanted to talk to her. I had tried to go slow on my drink but it was finished.

Two more men came in, crew from the port with the name of a shipping company across the backs of their jackets. "Busy today?" one of them said, joking, as they dumped their jackets in a familiar way onto a chair near the pool table.

She smiled, making her way back behind the bar with her lit cigarette. They glanced at me, leaned on the bar with their heavy arms, took in the bartender, and then took their beers over to the pool table.

I wanted another drink. Before I could say anything the bartender came around to sit on one of the bar stools and watch the men play, pulling an ashtray close. I didn't want to leave my stool and let any of them see my rubber boots—which, it occurred to me, were a ridiculous thing to wear, even to a test. I took a sip of the melted ice water, realizing I was thirsty, and watched as the two men prepared for their game, putting the shiny pool balls onto the felt, rubbing blue chalk on the ends of their cues.

One of them had his head closely shaved and the other was wearing a baseball cap. They didn't talk to each other, but they were comfortable together, like brothers—or maybe, I thought, like all men are when they have something to concentrate on, like my father and Mr. Blackwell, cooking. One of them broke the triangle of tightly packed balls with a loud crack and they both patrolled the table, considering their next moves.

The bartender sighed. "You need another?" she said, turning to me. When I nodded she got reluctantly to her feet. "I'm supposed to be done with my shift now," she said to no one in particular.

Her replacement showed up a minute later, a man I recognized from town. He had a handlebar mustache and big bushy eyebrows. His children went to Yvesport Elementary and I had seen him dropping them off. Mr. Blackwell knew him. "I didn't think you were going to show up," she said to him, filling a glass with ice water and bringing it to me absently.

I took a sip anyway, glad to have it, though I couldn't tell if this meant she wasn't going to give me another whiskey.

The new bartender was checking the inside of the refrigerator. "She need something?" he said, nodding at me.

"Whiskey," she said, opening another beer for herself. "I'm getting it. On the house," she said quietly after she put it down, lifting her beer in a little toast before she took a swig and sat down next to me.

"Thanks," I said, lifting my own drink awkwardly and nearly missing my mouth.

"Slow today?" said the other bartender.

"The usual. That asshole who gets the Chivas came in."

He wasn't looking at her. He brought in new ice and then started picking up the glasses on the shelf and squinting at them like they might be dirty.

"You from around here?" she said, turning to me.

"Crab Island," I said.

She shrugged as if she wouldn't have cared even if she did know where it was. "I'm not from here," she said.

"It's between here and Campobello," I said. I couldn't remember the last time someone had asked me where Crab Island was. You could see it from the breakwater. "Where are you from?"

She shrugged again. "Arizona, sort of. My mom lives on the reservation."

Before I knew it I was glancing up at her face, searching for the telltale cheekbones, Mr. Blackwell's turned-down mouth. "She's only half Indian," she said, with a wry smile, "but she gets money from the government anyway. I actually look more Indian than her, because of my hair." She motioned at my whiskey with her cigarette. "Is that your lunch?"

"Not really." I blushed.

She looked straight at me for a minute, and then took another drag of her cigarette. "Not like there's anything else to do around here," she said, looking back at the pool table.

I looked at the men too, not sure how to respond. I had been under the impression that everyone in Yvesport had plenty to do. They were all busy, with their tests and boyfriends and basketball games and bra shopping. And I had my chores and going back and forth every day and dinner to cook. But I knew this was not what she meant. "I was supposed to take a test today," I said. "For college."

"What happened?" she said, putting out her cigarette and picking up her beer.

"I didn't feel like it."

She laughed, a kind of snort of agreement. "I hate tests," she said.

I thought of the woods, and wished I could think of something else to say. I was quiet again.

She looked at me. "I'm getting another beer. Do you know how to play pool?"

"No," I said.

"Let's go play with those guys," she said. "You want to? I'll get you another whiskey."

I must have forgotten about my boots by then, because the next thing I knew we were walking over to the pool table. She went to sit on the radiator and patted the metal beside her to indicate that I should sit down too. I perched on the end, holding my whiskey. The two men were concentrating on their game but after she got them fresh beers they looked more interested, and she introduced us. Her name was Susie. Soon I was learning to play pool, and they were drinking more beers, and one of the men, the one with the hat, was telling me about the supertanker they were on, which was being loaded at Estes Head. They were headed for China after they finished in the United States, and would be let off the ship for only one day at each port. It would take twenty-nine days to cross the ocean.

I looked over at Susie, who was talking to the other man, and suddenly she was laughing, her face flushed. She looked younger, and maybe even a little shy, one hand in her jeans pocket as she listened.

"Have you ever been to China?" said my sailor.

"No," I said, "have you?"

He nodded. "Been there for a day."

"A day?"

"That's all we get," he said. "Most of the guys go into town." He lifted up his cap as if to cool off from the thought of what they did there, and I saw his hair underneath, short, but not shaved. "But I like to try to see some things. People around the harbor. They have these boats called junks with square sails."

I nodded, wondering if I was on my third or fourth whiskey.

Somehow we'd ended up by the bar; he must have bought me another drink. He told me he was thinking of building a boat at home, and when he'd drawn the shape of it in the sand in China the man with the junk had drawn the shape of his hull too, and like that they had communicated.

Susie came up alongside me, as if to tell me a secret. "They want to show us their boat." Before I could answer she had slipped behind the bar and was gathering her jacket and keys. When she came back out she was grinning. She showed us a full bottle of whiskey under her jacket. "Come on," she said, looking at me. "It'll be fun."

Her sailor took the whiskey so that she could put on her jacket—denim, lined with wool but not nearly warm enough for October weather. She pulled her ponytail out from the back and shook it out with a little pride. "I bet you've never been on a supertanker before," she said to me.

Her sailor looked pleased. "I know the guy doing security tonight," he said to his friend as we made our way toward the door.

I found my jacket on the bar stool and pulled it queasily over my head, hurrying to catch up. The bar had grown murky and warm with sound as more people had come in, and I felt them watching us leave. Outside it was still raining, and the parking lot seemed huge, the town on the hill above us sinking into the afternoon. I was drunk and concentrated on getting across the parking lot. Susie told the men to get in the back of her car and I stood there swaying as they climbed inside.

The car lurched into the rain, and the men passed the

whiskey back and forth. I wondered if I might be sick. Someone shouted about music and the car filled with noise. Susie concentrated on the road. She drove straight down to the security check, where a man in uniform peered into the car and laughed at us. It was getting dark as we drove down to the loading docks, empty and lit with yellowish lights. Susie took the whiskey when we got out of the car and tipped it up into her mouth. The iron flanks of the supertanker rose up above her into the fog. I looked up toward the lights on the deck, softened by the mist, and felt my mind sharpen in fear. She wiped her mouth and passed me the whiskey and I drank.

We had to go up the gangplank single file. It was like climbing a long ladder. Susie and her sailor went first, giddy and eager, and my sailor stayed behind, helping me with the steps. When we got to the top I walked out to the nearest railing. There was a metal coaming at chest height and I leaned against it and looked down, not at the water but at the dock below us—a tangle of pumps and gas pipes—and began to vomit.

My sailor was kind; he kept the hair out of my face and rubbed my back through my raincoat. He led me to the foredeck to get a glass of water. I forgot Susie in the dazzle of fluorescent lights; soon there were more metal stairs and then his bedroom, with steel walls, a TV fixed high in one corner. It was as big as any bedroom, I thought as I pulled off my wet jacket and lay down. It even had a window—square, not round. My sailor sat on the edge of the bed murmuring things, touching my hair. I took off my boots and they wiggled to the floor. Then I took off my wool sweater, and my T-shirt with it, and he leaned forward and kissed my breasts through the thin cloth of my bra. I looked at his smooth haircut, the motion of his big head as he pushed up my bra to put his mouth on my nipples. He seemed far away and I felt tall, like my neck was longer than I had ever imagined. He is all the way down there kissing me, I thought, and I'm all the way up here. Alone. When he came back up to kiss my mouth he kept missing. I wanted to get inside him, to get in his throat and burrow down into him. I undid his belt and reached for his penis, which sprang stiffly from his pants, but felt rubbery and strange in my hand.

I wasn't sure what to do with it—I worked myself down on the bed and tried to put it in my mouth but it was too big and I was afraid I would bite him. He got my jeans off somehow, and then he was on top, inside me, looking down with a kind of shocked expression. The ceiling above us was metal. I moved back and forth with him, awkwardly, to feel more of him inside me, and then suddenly he pulled out and came all over my stomach. We lay there until we heard someone running in the corridor, and my sailor sat straight up and told me to put on my clothes. My whole body was like liquid, my stomach sticky and wet, and when I stood up the room swung out of focus.

He helped me put my pants back on, and then my socks and my boots, as if I was a child. "You okay?" he said gently.

His friend pounded on the door. "Greg! You gotta get her outta here." When he opened the door his friend was standing there smiling. "Rinaldi saw me," he said.

My sailor put on his shirt and next thing I knew he was walking me back to the stairway. I held my coat in a tight bundle against my stomach and went down step by step, afraid to look up and see if Susie's car was gone from the parking lot.

She was waiting for me with her headlights on. I could see her smoking a cigarette in the driver's seat when I got close enough, and she leaned over to unlock the door.

"Did you get caught?" she said when I sat down, putting the cigarette in her mouth to handle the stick shift.

"Not really," I said, not sure what she meant.

She laughed again, that same derisive snort. "Either you did or you didn't."

"Well, they told me someone was coming," I said. It didn't seem like the right thing to be talking about. I felt sticky and strange, and I couldn't tell if the same thing had happened to her. I wanted to ask, but something told me it was not allowed. We were both silent as we turned down the road toward McMann's.

"Do you think you could drop me off at the town dock?" I finally said.

She rolled down the window just enough to drop out her cigarette. "You can stay at my house if you want."

"That's okay. My father'll be waiting for me."

She snorted again, a little exhale of breath, and I looked over at her. She was looking angrily out at the road, her eyes shining in the dark.

"What?" she said, when she felt me looking.

I didn't tell her that my father wouldn't be waiting, or that he would be asleep on the couch and have no idea where I had been. I didn't tell her that I'd never done anything like that before. I just said "nothing," the way I thought she would have, and turned to look out my window. I felt like I could hear our stories inside us like noise.

When she finally dropped me off I said goodbye as if I didn't care and slammed the door. But even as she drove away I didn't believe I would never see her again. It was not until I was driving the boat back across the water that it occurred to me that I had finally met someone who was more lonely than me.

9

Julie and Donna both scored well on the test; in the spring Julie got into Bowdoin and Donna got into the University of Maine. Anne Marie Gleason, who was also in our class, got pregnant and didn't show up for graduation. Mr. Blackwell mentioned it the one time he saw me in the spring. He said he thought she had it coming. I knew the chances were high that someone he knew had seen me that afternoon at McMann's, and sometimes I wondered if he knew. I didn't see the bartender around town, though I saw her car in the parking lot of McMann's almost every day on my way home from school that spring.

After school finished, Mr. Blackwell asked me if I wanted to work for him at the boatyard. I knew he'd hired boys from the high school every spring, but I had never known him to hire a girl. He'd never once asked if I was interested. It had been the same with the fishing, even when he had his own boat, though he knew perfectly well that I had never done anything during the summer but garden and cook for my father.

I almost said no, just to see if it would make him angry. But the thought of being able to see him every day was too tempting. It hadn't occurred to me that I needed to make money. I considered myself thrifty—more for the sake of efficiency than anything else—but my father had always given me the money I asked him for, whether it was for groceries or school supplies or a new steel ramp to be fitted on the pier, and I had never given much thought to where it came from. There was very little temptation in Yvesport for anything but the necessities.

"What sorts of things will you be doing for him?" my father asked when I told him that night at dinner.

"I don't know," I said. "Probably painting, mostly."

"I should think you could find a better way to spend your time."

I suppose I'd anticipated that he wouldn't like the idea: I'd made his favorite haddock that night with a sauce I knew he liked, using the black olives he'd had shipped from New York, along with my own canned tomatoes and garlic from the garden just to please him.

"It's only for the summer," I said.

"I see," he said, reaching for his drink. "And then I suppose you have a much better plan?"

I watched him take a sip, not sure how to reply. He was smiling, as if he was only teasing, but I could tell he was as surprised as I was at the way it had come out, a cruel spark.

He'd been disappointed when I had told him I'd missed the admissions test and the deadline for college applications, but he hadn't had any suggestions about what to do about it. Secretly, I thought it was possible he didn't want me to leave the island anyway. I had been busy that spring, getting the garden ready for summer, quietly taking the exams they gave us at the end of school, and I had been looking forward, in my own way, to settling in for another winter. I had won first prize in the art contest at school, for a drawing of a narcissus flower with its head drooping toward the ground, and I'd taken off the ribbon before I brought it home and given it to my father without telling him. He hung it in the living room, and I'd thought vaguely that I might draw other myths too, and one day surprise him with a set of illustrations for his work.

That night after supper I went for a walk. Mr. Blackwell had cut a path around the perimeter of the island and along the cliff at the back, and I knew each step of the way, day or night. Sometimes I'd try to trick myself, pretend I was in a new place: I'd look hard at the crag of the apple tree, or at the boulder that stood out at low tide, and try not to recognize it. But every turn and curve on the island was always more familiar, and before I knew it I'd be home, back in time for bed, or breakfast, or dinner.

I stood for a long time looking at the bay. I often wondered if my mother had done this before the day she left the safety of the island and got lost. It was easy, even in the dark, to see the shape of the bay and each jut of land; heading straight out of our cove in almost every direction but one would have brought the boat to shore. In any case, my father had let her go. And so had I. But wasn't it also possible that she had wanted to escape? She must have been lonely. Mr. Blackwell had never said she was happy, and the only thing people in town seemed to remember about her was that she was shy.

I started work for Mr. Blackwell before the end of June. Though the lot was crammed full of boats in the winter, it was nearly empty in the summer, except for the few old schooner hulls the trade school was working on, suspended in midair like spacecrafts. There wasn't much painting to do, since any boat that wasn't in need of heavy repair was in the water. Instead, despite my apologies for my math skills, Mr. Pinter had me doing the books, which consisted of recording and adding up wads of yellow receipts he'd collected during the spring. Three boys from school were helping Mr. Blackwell rebuild an old sardine carrier that Butch Harris was planning to use for whale-watching tours. I watched them from the window of the trailer Mr. Pinter used as his office, climbing up and down ladders in the sun, walking across the deck of the huge white hull while I shuffled through wrinkled papers and mildewed files.

I had only been working there for a week when I came home one night to find the other dory missing. It had been a while since my father had gone into town by himself and I felt immediately irritated by it. Guessing he might be late for supper, I started cooking fried scallops, his least favorite dish. But as it started to get dark I remembered Mr. Blackwell had told me a hurricane was brewing southeast of Florida, and I found myself going out twice to be sure the porch light was on. It had begun to rain. Finally I made a custard pie, out of guilt for cooking him such a punishing meal. By the time he came through the door I had a glass of whiskey ready, and reheated the scallops, and put everything out on the table as if I had only just gotten around to it.

He ate quickly, as if he was hungry, and didn't seem to notice how cold the scallops were in the center, or that they were scallops at all. "I spoke to Walter today," he said finally, unable, it seemed, to contain his excitement. "They need your help at the institute."

"Who's Walter?" I asked.

"He runs the institute," he said. "In New York."

"The institute?" I repeated.

"Arthur's institute," he said impatiently. "The Institute for Classical Studies, with the library I set up. They need someone right away."

I looked at him. "In New York?"

"That's right," he said, reaching for his whiskey. "I think it might be good for you."

I felt my stomach tighten. "What if I don't want to go?" I said.

"Then you don't have to."

We were both quiet. I stared at my half-eaten scallops. "I made you a custard pie," I said, my voice small.

"Thank you," he said, smiling.

"How long would I have to go for?"

"Just a few weeks. Or as long as you want. Walter said they have a room you can stay in."

I stood up and went to get the pie. "We may need to prepare for a storm," I said, absently.

"A storm?" he said, watching me.

"Mr. Blackwell said there's something brewing near Florida." I put the pie down on the table between our plates, unable to look at him, and sat back down.

He nodded at my plate. "Somebody's not ready for dessert," he said gently.

The fog was thick as I drove across to the boatyard the next morning, steering by my compass the whole way. As I walked across the tarmac where the boats were stored in the winter the sound of someone hammering was ringing hard in the dampness. I went toward it, but it was one of the boys, and when I asked if Mr. Blackwell was there yet he shrugged. I went into the office. From the window I could see Mr. Blackwell talking to someone down at the fuel dock.

It was all I could do to wait until his eleven-thirty break—one of the boys was always around, hoping to have lunch with him, and I wanted to get him alone. I watched him climb up into Jim Craig's scallop boat, where he was redoing the floorboards. At eleven-fifteen I made a fresh pot of coffee, poured two cups, and walked down to him.

He took off his hat, pushing a hand through his sweaty black hair. "You telling me it's time for a break?" he said, looking down at me over the edge of the boat.

"My dad found a job for me in New York City," I said, looking up at him.

He smiled. "Is that right?" He put his hat back on and I saw him cast a glance over his work before he went over to the ladder to climb down to me.

I was nearly as tall as he was when he was on level ground. He took the cup of coffee and gestured toward the picnic bench in the weeds by the old loading dock.

"He says they need my help at the institute he used to work for," I said, when we'd both had a sip.

He nodded thoughtfully. "That'll be nice," he said.

"You think so?"

He shrugged. "How long you going for?"

"However long I want, I guess," I said.

"Might be good for you," he said. "Seeing things."

When I didn't answer he glanced over at me. "You're not gonna miss anything around here you know. Your dad'll just keep writing that book."

I nodded, my eyes filling with tears, and we both looked out at the foggy glare. I was glad to be sitting with him. I sniffed but he didn't look over; he was giving me my privacy, but I knew he was thinking of my father too.

"You two preparing for the storm?" he said finally, finishing his coffee. "It's a ways off, but it's supposed to be a big one. There's no guarantee that it won't get up here."

On my way back through town after work, indulging my melancholy, I stopped at the hardware store for storm supplies, though I had long since bought enough canned goods and emergency candles to make it through several winters. I liked the smell of Hardwick's: the burnt tar of the twine, the fresh white of new canvas and spools of untouched line, the bright rubber of the marine supplies. I bought some batteries and a few extra cotter pins for the outboard—it was one of the only repairs my father knew how to handle—and as I was putting them down on the counter it occurred to me that I was getting ready to leave.

"You see the people in Florida on TV?" Mr. Burns said as he rang them up. No one in Yvesport ever remembered that we didn't have a television.

"No," I said, "but Mr. Blackwell said it was pretty far off."

"Those people in Florida don't know where they are if they're not sitting in a traffic jam, trying to get somewhere. I suspect they'll all finish evacuating and come back home just in time for the storm to hit." He chuckled to himself.

I carried my bag down to the boat and as I headed over to the island, which was still emerging sleepily from the fog, I found myself wishing that I was already gone—the storm done with, my life changed. My father looked up in surprise as I came through the door and dropped my package on the counter.

"I guess I'll leave before the storm," I said to him as I unpacked the batteries and lined them up in the kitchen drawer. "Mr. Blackwell said it's a ways off."

10

There was a lot to do in the week before I left, and I was glad for it. Although the rumors of the storm's force were subsiding, it gave everyone a sense of urgency, and people responded to my various requests with unusual efficiency. Even though it was still August, Sam Ames brought over enough cords of wood to last my father through Christmas and helped me pile it on the hill behind the house, in case the water rose during the storm; Mrs. Malloch said she'd send her grandson over to cut the grass while I was gone. I spent several mornings on my knees preparing the flower beds in front of the porch, though Mr. Blackwell said he'd be over to do some weeding "while my father had his nose in his books."

I made lists of instructions for my father to follow for the garden (tomatoes will give when ready) and the house (check generator switch when lights are out), restocked the kerosene and matches, cleaned the lamps, washed the blankets I had stored since spring. I made jam and froze berries, I cooked beans and restocked our store of potatoes and onions. We hardly spoke, but he drank very little and watched my frenzy of activity with a strange kind of contentment. Once I tried on the dresses Julie had given me and asked him to pick which one I should bring.

"Why can't you bring them all?" he said uncomfortably when I came downstairs with the first one on.

"They're only for formal occasions," I said, as if I knew better.

"What else are you bringing?" He looked at me reluctantly.

"Jeans, I guess. And sweaters."

He dropped his eyes. "I'm sure that one'll be fine," he said. "The color suits you."

"Do you think the shoulders are too tight?" I pushed.

"I think they're fine," he said, looking at me as if it hurt his eyes.

I went upstairs and took off the dress, embarrassed, not sure what I had wanted. I laid it down beside the others, and then hastily rolled up two of them and stuffed them into the duffel bag. Cool salty air came through the window and I felt tall and female in my bra and underwear. I peered at the picture of my mother on my desk. She always looked the same, smiling in a fixed way, like people do when they have portraits taken, as if they are holding themselves in. No matter what kind of mood I was in I could never make the picture come alive—she seemed to know I was looking at her, and stared back eerily, like one of Julie's dolls. I put my loose flannel shirt back on and the carpenter pants I'd been wearing in the garden. I hadn't meant to frighten him.

The storm finally came the morning I was leaving. Most people had left their boats in—it was only supposed to amount to a small-craft warning. The sky was dark, with a tint of the peculiar yellow that indicates the pressure lifting with the light.

The bay was ominously calm. My father's duffel bag barely tipped the dory. He waited politely for me to put a hand on the dock before he stepped in after me. Mr. Blackwell used to joke that it was his big brain that threw him off balance, and he still couldn't get into a small boat without pitching it.

The engine choked and then roared on the high throttle—I brought it down low and sat down behind him. I tried to think of something to say as we headed out of the cove but found myself waiting until we were out of range of the house; shadowy sky flashed in the panes of the living room windows, but the island already looked indifferent and still. I'd forced him to make a list of all the things he needed in town while we were sitting at the breakfast table, but I knew there would be something missing when he came back home without me.

"You have your list?" I yelled at him as the ocean hardened beneath the boat's speed. He turned around and gave me a nod, his gray hair blowing up in the wind. The bay lay behind us, some of the dark clouds edged now with rain. I thought of the foul-weather gear in my bag, though by the look of it I'd be in the bus by the time the storm started. When I slapped the channel marker for good luck as we passed, he didn't turn to give me his reproachful look.

The boats in the harbor jangled and bobbed in our wake. Most of the fishermen who were still working had left hours earlier, but the gulls were still wheeling around, unsettled among the rigs and masts, wary of the strange sky. Mr. Blackwell was waiting on the dock.

"Big day," he called out, as if to break the silence with my father before we got to the dock.

I shut off the motor and he came to help me onto the dock. "You two have time for some coffee?" he asked, nervously including my father.

"We ought to make sure we get a ticket," my father said, without meeting his eye. I looked back and forth between them.

"Won't keep the big-city girl waiting," Mr. Blackwell said, giving me a wink.

Before I could stop him my father shouldered the duffel bag, as if he always carried it, and began to walk up the ramp. I knew it was too heavy for him, and Mr. Blackwell knew it too. When we got to his truck in the breakwater parking lot my father looked away, and suddenly Mr. Blackwell was folding me in a hug. His rag wool sweater smelled of sweat and engine fuel.

"You take care now," he whispered in my ear.

My father glanced at us, and then he began walking down Main Street. Mr. Blackwell got into his truck and gave me a few farewell honks before he headed over to the boatyard.

They sold the tickets to Bangor at the drugstore. We bought one even though the bus wasn't coming for another hour, and then my father suggested, unexpectedly, that we go to the diner for some coffee.

We took two stools at the counter, and the waitress gave us each a mug and filled it with coffee before we asked. My father poured cream into his and then stirred it rapidly, so that the spoon rang against the sides. We could see the grill from our seats, and we watched the hash browns being shoved around. After a few minutes he got out a bank envelope and gave it to me. It was heavy as a chocolate bar, tight with cash. "I'm hoping that'll keep you," he said, "however long you're there."

It rained a little outside and I felt how small we were, in our little diner, in our little town. I could hear the wind against the windows, and suddenly everything felt unfamiliar. My father looked stooped beside me. I put my hand over his, noticing the brown spots, the wrinkled skin. His knuckled fingers were cool, and my own hand felt hot and clammy. I studied the napkin dispenser, coming untucked, a torn sugar packet beside it, lying in the dust of its contents. The room seemed queerly still.

"Maybe we should go," he said, giving my hand a quick squeeze, and then stood up, as if he had been sitting for hours.

We walked together to the bus station. He kissed me on the cheek as I got on, but he was gone before I found a seat. I saw him out the window, walking away, though I'd planned on waving to him. As the bus jerked and tilted out of town, past the high school playing field, past the new electrical plant and on toward the interstate, I wished he'd stayed just a moment longer. As if, in our life together, that was all we'd ever gotten wrong.

the age of bronze

11

The rain was pouring down in sheets when we arrived at the Port Authority bus terminal. A line of open umbrellas collected at the taxi stand outside, and people rushed from the brightly lit entrance out into the dark, bent over, holding newspapers above their heads. Gusts of wind fluttered the shop awnings and slowed the river of cars down the glittering avenue.

I got in line in my old rain jacket, still stiff with salt, my father's duffel bag on my shoulder. Eventually I was ushered to a taxi. It smelled like cigarettes inside. The driver moved through a confusion of shining bumpers into the traffic, banked on every side by windowed buildings, blinking storefronts. He was listening to another language on the radio. We turned off the avenue and the scale of the buildings shifted; there were trees. We clanked over the lid of a manhole and came to a stop. In the dark behind the sheets of rain I could make out the façade I had long since memorized in the photo of my father with Arthur Mitchell—the arched windows, the stout brownstone steps. I might as well have been stepping back into that same photograph.

"This it?" said the driver, to remind me he was waiting to be paid.

After he left I was standing uncertainly at the bottom of the rainy steps when someone opened the front door. A man in a white T-shirt looked up at the rain with an irritated glance, light pouring out of the doorway around him. He called something out to someone inside and began to fumble with his umbrella. It was the automatic kind, with a button on the handle, and something was stuck; I approached the steps, hoping he'd notice me.

"Fuck," he said, frowning at the umbrella. He was wearing glasses, and behind them I could see his long, thick lashes.

"Excuse me," I said finally. "I'm looking for the Institute for Classical Studies."

He glanced at my duffel bag. "Are you looking for someone in particular?"

"Who are you talking to?" The door opened wider and an older man in a silk robe and slippers came into the vestibule and looked out. Despite his outfit he carried himself with the kind of exaggerated formality that my father did after a few whiskeys, and my first impression was that he might be drunk. "What have we here?"

"I'm looking for the Institute for Classical Studies," I repeated, as if it was the only sentence I knew. I moved the duffel bag in closer to me so that it wouldn't get too soaked.

"Well, don't just stand there drowning," said the older man. "Help her with her bag, Nathaniel."

Nathaniel started gingerly down the steps toward me, but I had already swung the bag onto my back and they both stepped aside to let me through. The entryway was dark and warm, and in those first dim moments, as I rested my damp bag on the worn Oriental carpet, I thought it looked very glamorous. An electric chandelier shone on the thick banister leading up the stairway to the second floor, and there was a framed mirror, spotted with age, on the opposite wall in which I could see myself, in my yellow coat, reflected like a flame in the murk.

"I suppose you're Peter Donnal's daughter," the older man said, studying my face.

"Yes," I said. "Are you Walter?"

"I'm Robert." He tightened his sash impatiently, and then, keeping his eyes on me, he went over to the stairs. "Miranda Donnal has arrived," he yelled upward.

In a minute another man was peering down at me. He looked about my father's age and was fully dressed, though his hair was tousled, as if he'd just gotten up from a nap. "How amazing," he said, staring at me quietly.

"He said he would send her," Robert said, looking back up at him.

"Well, I didn't expect her to look exactly like him," the other man said as he came down the stairs. He took both my hands in his and smiled at me like a priest. "I'm Walter," he said, gently, as if I might disappear. "We're very happy to have you." My hands were cold and I saw him glance at my dripping jacket. "She's soaked!" he said to Robert. "How did you get here, by boat?"

"By bus," I said, smiling.

"Goodness. Well, take off your coat and stay awhile." He

dropped my hands and looked at the others. "We should take you to the club or something. Shouldn't we? Nathaniel can come too."

I had to pull my jacket over my head, and for a moment I was in the dark and struggling to get out, and then I surfaced in the cool air, and they were all looking at me. I pulled at the hem of my skirt to unwrinkle it, and tried to hold my wet jacket away from me.

"Amazing," said Walter, shaking his head.

"She's his daughter, after all," Robert said.

Nathaniel was tapping his umbrella against his thigh. "I have to go meet my sister," he said, apologetically.

Robert smirked and looked at me. "You wouldn't want to get in the way of Nathaniel's sister."

"I'm sure you two will have plenty of time to meet," Walter said.

Nathaniel gave me a little nod, sort of a bow, as Robert showed him out. "See you," he said, earnest.

"You must be starving," said Walter, turning to me with a smile. "Should I get you a drink? Or maybe I should show you your room and then we can all go out."

"The club's a little extravagant for a Sunday night, isn't it?" Robert commented, wandering over to poke at a pile of mail on the hall table.

Walter looked at him. "You're not actually passing up an opportunity to go to the club, are you?"

Robert kept his back to us. "It's not like I haven't got anything else to do."

Walter rolled his eyes at me, as if to indicate that he was used to this, and gestured for me to follow him upstairs. The library, classroom, and office was downstairs, he was saying, and the bedrooms were upstairs. My duffel bag kept brushing against the cracked paint on the wall, and each time a few green chips wheeled into the air. Walter was explaining breathlessly that the after-school Latin classes Robert ran during the school year were starting tomorrow, and that Robert had hired Nathaniel to help him out because so many boys had enrolled. Robert also wrote theater reviews, and Walter said the "transition" between the two jobs was often difficult for him, though he would do nothing but go out to shows all year long anyway.

My room was in the back, down at the end of a short hallway. "We've been thinking of renting this room for years," he said, opening the door for me, "but someone always needs a place to stay, and it's the perfect guest room."

I squeezed past him and sat down involuntarily on the bed. The walls were the same fading green as the rest of the house— though better preserved, as if from being hidden away. The ceiling slanted down toward the garret window at the back and a small desk fit in one corner. It was decorated with a bouquet of flowers, now dead.

"We can get rid of these," Walter said, walking over to pick up the vase. A few of the dried leaves fell to the floor, making a scratchy sound. "And I'll get you some fresh sheets. You make yourself comfortable."

"Thank you," I said from the bed.

"We'll be waiting downstairs," he said. His eyes searched my face again, and he smiled. "It has been a long time, hasn't it?" he said.

I heard him going down the hall and then his footsteps back down the stairs. In the quiet I could feel the lurch of my lost momentum. I sat there for a minute, staring at the window, until I heard the rain, pattering against it. I had to bang on the window sash a few times with the base of my palm before it would open. The wet drops glittered in the dark. The brick wall of another building was a few feet away; a stream of water ran down from the gutter beside the window, offering a thick, silvery escape-route. I reached out to touch it and it broke apart, shattering noisily in the alley below before I took my hand away and it went smooth again.

Robert and Walter were waiting for me in the cluttered kitchen, sipping from teacups without saucers. Walter had put on a blazer; Robert had changed into white trousers and a sand-colored jacket and tie. Most of the clutter, I realized, looking around, was newspapers in haphazard piles, tilting off the refrigerator, piled on the chairs and counters. Buried behind them was an antique stove upon which someone had put a coffee machine and a toaster, the only evidence that the kitchen was in use at all.

"Scotch?" said Walter, lifting his teacup inquisitively.

I shook my head and then instantly changed my mind.

"Shall we go then?" said Robert, standing up. They both deposited their cups onto a pile of twenty or so in the sink. They seemed used to the dim light in the lobby, and they both found their umbrellas in the shadows. I thought of my jacket and was hesitating, ready to run upstairs, when Walter popped his umbrella open on the steps and held an arm out for me.

I had to stoop to get under it, but I was glad to hold his arm once we were outside. People rushed by hurriedly; once we turned onto the bigger avenue, cars passed continually, their tires making a sticking sound in the rain. Lights were on everywhere and all the surfaces of all the windows and sidewalks were flashing with headlights. It seemed as if no one had gone inside since I had arrived, they'd just kept hurrying in the streets, clustering in doorways.

We turned onto another, quieter street, like the one the institute was on, where the buildings huddled close again, and Walter steered me toward a soggy flag with a peacock on it. I could feel the side of my dress getting damp. We went up the steps and they folded their umbrellas discreetly. "Your father will be very jealous," Walter said happily as we went inside. "You have to tell him we took you here."

Inside it was more like a hotel than a restaurant, and it seemed empty at first, but out of nowhere a man in a dark green jacket came and took the umbrellas, and they all nodded as if they knew each other, or didn't—I couldn't tell. Robert led us down a small set of stairs whose walls were crowded with little ink sketches of men in top hats with captions like "Spring in Washington Square." At the bottom was the dining room, filled with candlelit tables, red curtains across the windows. A large stuffed peacock, with a long blue-and-gold feather tail, tilting to one side on its wire feet, was mounted on a pedestal at the entrance.

"Gentlemen!" Another man in a green jacket came gliding toward us. "It's been *far* too long." He kissed Robert and Walter on their cheeks, and then tilted his head as if he was imitating the bird. "And who is this beautiful young lady?"

Walter smiled. "Peter Donnal's daughter," he said gently,

putting a hand on my shoulder. The man looked from me to Walter and Robert and then did a little pantomime of amazement, his hands on either side of his face. "Isn't it amazing?" Walter said, proudly. "Gerry was a great fan of Arthur's," he said to me.

"And your father's," Gerry corrected him.

"Do you think we can have their table?"

"Absolutely," Gerry said, looking toward the back of the room. He plucked three menus from the shelf beside him and gestured for us to follow. Bursts of quick and chattery talk erupted out of the murmur and clink of silverware as we passed each table. It was mostly men, I noticed, with a few women, thin and lustrous, like photographs from a magazine.

Gerry pulled a chair out for me. "Do you want to try the merlot?" he asked Walter, as I made discreet little hops to try to bring my chair in closer. Before I knew it a waiter was behind me pushing me in tight. There were waiters everywhere, wearing white coats, moving in and out of the candlelight like moths.

Walter and Robert were unfolding their napkins, looking around with evident satisfaction. "We used to come here with Arthur all the time," Walter said, watching Gerry come back toward us.

Gerry showed him the label on the bottle, then poured a splash into Robert's wineglass, so tall and light that it seemed the weight of the red wine would break it.

"Your father must have taught you all about wine," Walter said, looking at me, as Robert took a sip and nodded at Gerry, who obediently filled all our glasses.

As far as I knew my father had never drunk anything but whiskey. I gave a modest shrug, keeping the contradiction to myself.

"To our beautiful guest," Walter said, raising his glass.

Gerry raised the bottle he was holding and winked at me. I caught a glimpse of my freckly forearm as I raised my glass too, and for a moment, I felt almost pretty. Behind Robert a woman threw back her head and laughed. I felt a glimmer of excitement breaking open in me.

"I've always wondered what Peter found for himself to eat up there," Walter said as he picked up his menu. "It's hard to imagine him surviving without his fois gras."

"We mostly cook ourselves," I said, not sure what he meant.

"Don't tell me Peter cooks," said Robert.

Walter gave him a look. "I should hope he does, dear. Miranda's mother passed away just after they got there and the two of them were on that island alone. Isn't that right?"

I nodded. Mr. Blackwell appeared before me at the stove, stirring the navy bean soup, holding up the spoon for my father to taste.

"What does he cook?" Robert asked, giving Walter a glance to get credit for the more polite tone.

More Mr. Blackwell, absently using a long knife to flip over a grilled cheese sandwich for me when we got back from school, a dish towel thrown over his shoulder. "A lot of things," I said, reaching for my wine. I couldn't remember the last time my father had cooked a meal himself.

"Like what?"

"Well—oatmeal," I said.

Robert raised his eyebrows and took a sip of his own wine.

"I suppose he must have had some help when you were young," Walter said with a reassuring smile.

"Not really," I said, feeling myself beginning to blush. I didn't know why I was lying. It would have been impossible, of course, for us to have done anything without Mr. Blackwell. "Sometimes a woman came over from town," I said, suddenly making things up. "But he learned pretty fast. We eat a lot of fish."

"He couldn't put caviar on a cracker when we knew him," Robert said lightly, picking up his menu as if he didn't want to hear any more about it.

"We don't do a lot of cooking either," Walter pressed on. "Unless you count toasting bagels. But maybe you'll change our ways."

"Do you both live at the institute?"

"Well, yes," said Walter, startled. "We live in Arthur's apartment. It's just down the hall from your room."

I could feel Robert watching me, and I picked up my menu and pretended to concentrate on it. So they lived together. It wasn't my fault that I didn't know anything about their life. They knew nothing about my life either. I could see that Robert was miffed, but he had been unpleasant with me from the start. It would have been obvious, if I had thought about it. They were lovers. My menu seemed to be written in a foreign language, and it added to my panic. I sensed, with a horrible vertiginous feeling, how many things I didn't understand—everything, it seemed. Suddenly I was clumsy. I was Miranda, wearing Julie's dress. A man appeared beside me and with long metal tongs lifted a small bread roll as if it was a lobster and placed it on the plate beside me. I reached for my wine and nearly knocked it over.

Walter recommended the steak and I ordered it even though I wasn't hungry, along with a salad, which they insisted on. Was it possible that my father had hated all my meals? *He couldn't put caviar on a cracker when we knew him.* Walter ordered another bottle of wine to go with the entrees, and I tried to tell myself to drink more slowly, but I kept gulping it down. It was only making me more nervous.

"So did your father ever have any visitors on that island of yours?" Robert asked, zeroing in again. "Or was it always just the two of you out there, forsaking the world?"

"He's working on a translation," I said. The wine was making my face hot and I could no longer tell if I was blushing. In Yvesport when I told people my father was working on a translation they always nodded gravely, as if I'd told them he was ill, and didn't ask any more questions. But Robert and Walter didn't bat an eye. "He's almost finished," I added.

"We heard you were doing his typing for him," Robert said, with another polite look, leaning back as the waiter put his salad in front of him. The plate was huge, with a little tuft of greens at the center. "He's going to miss you, isn't he?" he said as he picked up his little fork. "That's very luxurious, having your daughter do all the typing and cooking. I suppose you were doing his laundry too?"

I jabbed at my salad. Who else would have done the laundry?

"Robert's a writer too," Walter said, as if that explained things.

"Well, not really," said Robert. "I write reviews. But it's not full time."

I didn't know what he was talking about, but I tried to give him the same polite look he kept offering me. The dining room was moving faster, or I was going slower. I had used the wrong fork for my salad, of course. I straightened my back, which was the only thing I could remember my father teaching me about good manners.

When the steaks came they had a little row of asparagus next to them, and I found myself telling Walter and Robert about how I'd tried to grow asparagus on the island, which wasn't really true. I'd ordered the seeds because my father had said it was the only vegetable he missed, but it had turned out that asparagus took five years to cultivate, and in the end I hadn't even tried planting them. I had always felt guilty about not having the patience to grow the only vegetable he ever said he wanted. At the time he hardly ever talked about New York, so it had made an impression on me, the fact that he missed the asparagus. And here I was, lying again.

"I told Miranda's father we could use some help putting the library card catalog on a database," Walter said to Robert. "Wouldn't that be great?"

"Mmm. Too bad nobody goes in there unless they're sleeping, or stealing something."

"Well, that's the point, dear. If we could make it available electronically then we could loan things to other libraries."

"I told you I was going to write one of those Landmark grants for that. We hardly need to lock the girl in the library."

"We're not locking her anywhere. It was her father's idea." He smiled at me. "He told me you can type faster than he can think."

I smiled back, though it was impossible to imagine my father saying something like that. My steak had begun to look like the walls of a big red cliff.

"Wasn't your mother a secretary?" said Robert. "I thought that was how they met."

"Was she?" Walter looked at him with interest.

"I think so," said Robert. He looked at me. "She was a great mystery, your mother. Depressed, I hear."

Walter was moving his leg under the table, trying to get Robert's attention. "Maybe we should get dessert," he said, looking around. "What was it that Arthur always got? That pastry?"

"The napoleon," Robert said.

Depressed? I looked at him, alert with anger, certain now that he was being mean on purpose. "Did you ever meet her?" I asked, as if I didn't care.

"I'm afraid I didn't," said Robert, looking back at me with his polite face. "We frankly didn't know she existed until your father moved to Maine with his wife and child."

"Well, we knew, of course, once he told us he was going," Walter broke in nervously. "You were, what—two or three years old? It's amazing to imagine how you've grown into such a— *person* since then, isn't it?"

I blinked. A person? I had no idea what it meant that Robert didn't know my mother existed, or why it mattered so much. It had been a long time since my mother existed for me too—in

fact I'd hardly ever imagined her at all. And now she was a secretary. I looked with sudden confusion at my hand on the stem
of my empty glass, strangely outsized. A waiter came and took
the order for dessert and coffee and both Walter and Robert
watched him walk away. I closed my eyes for a minute, wishing I
wasn't so confused, and when I opened them again another
waiter was there, putting a tiny cup down in front of me.

It was doll-sized, filled with what looked like a few table-
spoons of dark coffee. I looked over at Walter, who calmly
picked up his tiny spoon and measured a tiny amount of sugar
into his tiny cup. Robert did the same. I looked into the little cup
and started to giggle.

Walter and Robert looked up in surprise, and the minute I
tried to stop giggling I could feel it changing to tears. "I'm
sorry," I said, trying to smile, my eyes filling. "These cups are
so small!"

"They are sort of ridiculous, aren't they?" Walter said, smiling, picking up his own cup and looking at it askance. He took a
sip with exaggerated daintiness, pursing his lips and batting his
eyelashes.

I kept giggling, even though I was also crying; tears rolled
down my cheeks. Robert looked at us innocently and then
picked up his tiny spoon and stirred it in his tiny cup, miming a
little tea party, before he quietly put the spoon inside his nose.

Walter and I burst into laughter, and finally I was really
laughing, tears still running down my face but my throat opening
at last. Walter took a few deep breaths and I did too, wiping my
eyes. The dessert came and Robert pushed it over to me.

It was a rectangular pastry, with a diamond pattern of chocolate traced in the white icing on the top. It sat like a small house in the middle of the plate, which was streaked with chocolate and dusted with sugar. I pushed the side of my fork into it and we all watched it capsize, the layers of custard and fine French pastry sliding out from one another, making a mess of the carefully decorated plate.

12

It was still raining when I woke up the next morning, and a damp, warm breeze was coming in from my open window. I lay there like a shipwrecked sailor for what seemed like hours, unable to open my eyes, until finally I heard gulls. I turned to see the ocean out the window, and found myself staring at the little desk where the dead flowers had been, my father's duffel bag propped against it, open from when I'd dug for my toothbrush the night before. The screech of brakes, eerie and far-off down the avenues, came through the window.

I put my face into my pillow, and the sheets smelled soapy but stale. At home my father would have been awake for hours, the whole house would smell of coffee, and the oatmeal would have grown cold. I got up and tried to get my clothes out of the duffel bag but they were packed in too tight, and the whole thing was damp. I turned it over to shake it out on the bed and everything came loose: the clothes, my sketch pads, the sneakers I had carefully scrubbed free of mud. I had packed a box of drawing tools, and it fell open, the contents rolling out onto the blanket: pieces of charcoal, drawing pencils scattering on the floor, the fountain pens my father had given me for each of my birthdays clacking heavily against each other. I picked them all up and put them back in the box, glad to have them. It took only minutes to put my clothes into the bureau drawers, which were lined with fragile old paper. I hung Julie's dresses in the closet and put on a pair of jeans.

Walter cleared some newspaper from the chair next to him when he saw me come through the door. "You're allowed to sleep in, you know," he said.

"Is it early?" I said nervously, glancing at the coffee machine plugged in on top of the old stove.

"*Some people* think it's early, don't they, Robert?" he said. "But I've had to be at the university by eight for the past five years, so I don't actually notice."

"*Some people* make it unpleasant to be awake," Robert answered, plucking a bagel from the toaster and wincing at the heat, dropping it onto his plate with an annoyed expression, as if it was the bagel's fault it was hot.

Walter sighed. "You'll be nice to our guest, right, and show her the library?"

I saw Robert's gaze snag for a moment on the spot of ink at the bottom of Walter's shirt pocket. "Are you coming to that dinner tonight?" he said.

Walter was buckling up his briefcase. He had a tie tucked into his pocket. "I was the one who invited you, remember? Is that boy of yours coming over today?"

"I should hope so," said Robert. "He's teaching a class."

Walter gave me a little wave before he left. "Good luck with school," he said to Robert as he turned away.

Robert poured me a cup of coffee and pushed it over. "I can't offer you oatmeal," he said, "but I can offer you your choice of a sesame or poppy seed."

"Thanks," I said, smiling. The coffee was watery and strange, but I was happy to have it anyway. Robert had on another pair of light cotton trousers, a yellow shirt. No matter what he was wearing, I thought, he seemed to feel he looked very well in it. My blue jeans were relatively new, and so was my blouse, but I had a feeling that no matter what I had put on that morning I would have felt out of place.

"I can never get enough coffee in these teacups," Robert mumbled, standing up to refill his cup.

"I think the coffee's a little weak," I said, without thinking.

For the first time since I had arrived, he smiled at me. "I know! It's terrible, isn't it?"

"Well, it's—"

"Walter keeps saying it's too strong. But I've told him," he said, sitting back down beside me. "I might as well be talking to a wall."

"Do you want me to make another pot?"

"Oh no," he waved his hand dismissively, smiling. "I'm just complaining. I like to get my espresso later in the morning anyway." He handed me my toasted bagel and passed over the cream cheese, watching as I spread it with the knife.

"You don't have to do all that typing, you know," he said. "We were supposed to get a grant for it."

"That's okay," I said. "I don't really have anything else to do."

"I imagine you'll find plenty to keep you occupied," he said.

I bit into my bagel, realizing that I hadn't once thought about what I would do when I got here. My father had said I had a job and it had seemed then that that was all I needed to know. But I hadn't thought about what it would be like not to be home, not to have breakfast with him, not to get in a boat to start my day. And certainly I hadn't thought about the institute, with its strange cluttered kitchen, my bedroom, and the long stairway my father must have gone up and down. I had seen the door to the library he had spoken of off the foyer.

"So you're opening your school today?" I said after a while.

Robert rolled his eyes. "It's just a few after-school classes, really. I had no idea they'd get so popular. I had to hire that graduate student to help me and he's very pretty but I have a feeling he's dumb as a post."

I was about to ask if he was referring to the man I'd met the day before when suddenly he appeared in the hallway, cheerfully striding toward us.

"Ah ha," said Robert. "If it isn't Mr. Stoddard."

Mr. Stoddard laughed and generously introduced himself to me again as Nate. He was dressed in khakis and a crisp shirt, an outfit not unlike Robert's. He dropped casually into Walter's vacant chair, stretching his long legs out in front of him. "How was the club?" he asked.

"It was alright," Robert said. "Full of old farts. We should take you there sometime so that everyone can have something to look at."

Nate laughed, evidently used to this kind of compliment. He

was pretty, I thought blearily, the way the summer people in Yvesport were handsome—like garden flowers—tanned and well-tended-for.

"How's your sister?" Robert asked him.

"She's on a diet," he said, "so she can fit into my mom's wedding dress."

"Hasn't she heard of a tailor?"

"Supposedly it's almost a perfect fit—my mother's taller, but all she has to do is take up the hem. I think they're sort of competitive about it."

"They'll have to let it back down when you get married then, won't they?"

Nate hesitated for a moment and then laughed again. "It'll probably be awhile," he said, with a blush. "I wouldn't want to upstage her."

Robert raised his eyebrows. "Neither would I," he said, taking a sip of his coffee. "And I've only met her once. What does she do again? Isn't she in fashion or something?"

"She works at an art gallery," Nate said. "You should come see it sometime," he said, turning to me. "It's actually pretty cool."

"Miranda's going to be very busy, unfortunately," said Robert. "She's come all the way to New York from Maine to put our library card catalog on a database."

Nate looked at me, his big gentle eyes trying to gauge my response. "I bet there's some pretty interesting stuff in there," he said encouragingly.

"It's actually her father's collection," Robert said a little irritably, getting up to put his cup on top of the pile in the sink. "He used to go on book-buying trips in Europe every summer with Arthur."

"No kidding," Nate said, glancing at me, a little bit pleased to have hit a nerve with Robert. "Sounds like a pretty good gig."

"Well, Miranda," Robert said, changing the subject, "I'm sorry it's raining for your first day in the big city. But I suppose your father's given you directions to all the most tedious museums."

"I don't mind the rain," I said, realizing I was being dismissed. I got up and took my cup to the sink.

"I'm having lunch with my sister tomorrow," said Nate, "if you want to come. We can check out the place she works."

I could feel Robert watching us. "Thanks," I said. "That would be nice." I turned to Robert awkwardly. "I guess I'll see you later," I said.

"I guess you will," said Robert, getting up for yet another cup of coffee.

Nate was the kind of boy Julie would have liked, I thought as I climbed the stairs. He was the kind of boy she hoped she would meet in college. I could hear Robert teasing him from all the way upstairs. I shut my door behind me, feeling as if it had already been days since I had been alone. I had put the money envelope my father had given me under the mattress, and when I pulled it out it seemed remarkably thin. But when I opened it the bill on top was a hundred. I looked at Benjamin Franklin's friendly face, not unlike Walter's, and I remember thinking that this was the currency here—the currency of New York City.

My jacket was on the banister where I'd left it, heavy and musty, and I put it over my head gratefully, like a coat of armor, and then put the hundred-dollar bill into the jacket's front pocket and pressed the rusty snap shut. It was warmer outside than I had expected, and as I was going down the steps I could tell I would be too hot. I kept going anyway, walking down the street the institute was on until I hit Eighth Avenue, full of people in perfectly pressed clothes with perfectly tailored raincoats and umbrellas, walking carefully around the puddles at the end of each sinking block. They seemed to feel as if the weather was meant for someone else, or somewhere else. I thought of my father—his fussiness, his half-distracted, half-purposeful walk, his mild hurry.

I walked across a bigger avenue and the shops extended as far as I could see: I walked past restaurants and bars, rows of small tables under dripping awnings waiting to be filled, shops with their doors open, bookstores and beauty parlors and supermarkets. Before I knew it, the neighborhood had changed again, and I was passing a tall white building, gigantic as a factory. I rounded a forlorn corner and realized it was a hospital. Inside people in white coats walked down shining, empty halls. It seemed to me as out of place as the weather, that amidst all the shops and restaurants and things city people did, they could get sick.

A siren screamed through the air, and an ambulance careened around the corner. A few bored attendants in green outfits came outside under the awning to meet it. I watched as it pulled into the dock and a stretcher was handed out the back. It disappeared with a knot of people through the swinging doors. In Yvesport when there was a siren it meant that someone at the nursing home was having trouble, and the next day nearly everybody knew who it was. I almost collided then with a man walking a very large dog; he looked at me as if it was my fault.

I was looking up the street, thinking I ought to turn around, when I spied an aluminum cart near the hospital entrance, its little awning sticking out over the sidewalk, with COFFEE written down the side of it in big enthusiastic letters. It looked familiar, like a boat pulled up at the dock, and I headed straight for it, as if I had come to the end of my journey. Someone was bending down behind the shelves of donuts. As soon as he saw me he straightened up and came to the window, his face flushed, rearranging his cap to cover a few loose curls.

"Can I have a cup of coffee, please?"

"Regular?" he said, plucking a paper cup from the top of the ridged stack beside him.

But he had a woman's voice, not a man's. His eyes were soft— *her* eyes were soft, a dark chocolaty brown. She was looking at me expectantly.

I had forgotten what she had asked. "Sorry?" I said, beginning to blush.

"Regular?" she said again, with less of an accent, thinking I had misunderstood her.

"Oh. Yes." I had no idea what she meant but my face had begun to broil. I tipped back my hood.

She reached for the plastic spoon she'd planted in the pail of sugar beside her and then dumped a heaping spoonful into the empty cup before she lifted it to the spigot. Her forearms were taut and muscular. Her other hand flipped open the valve on the big tank of coffee in front of her. When it was full she turned and hefted a full gallon of milk, bringing the contents of the cup to just below the brim in one splash.

I watched her press down on the plastic lid with her stout brown hand and when she asked if I wanted anything else I could think of nothing to say. I looked vaguely at the shelves through the gray Plexiglas.

"Bagels, rolls, donuts, muffins," she said, following my eyes. "For donuts I have chocolate, jelly, plain—and those ugly ones." She leaned out the window and pointed to a few of them, sitting on the shelf. "They don't have holes."

I laughed. They *were* ugly—ridged and shapeless, the dough a blotchy mix of chocolate and plain, thickly coated with glazed sugar.

"They're called crullers," she said, resting her elbows on the sill, looking at me. "And I don't recommend the honey glaze. A little soggy at this time of day. Chocolate's a tiny bit crispier."

"Oh!" I said. "Chocolate then."

"Your choice," she smiled. She reached for a square of wax paper to take the donut off the shelf and then put it neatly into a paper bag with the coffee. She watched as I rummaged in the pockets of my jeans, and then I remembered my stupid hundred-dollar bill, tucked in my coat.

"That's a nice coat," she said as I pulled out the bill and gave it to her. She stretched it open, giving it a quick glance before she reached into her own pocket and pulled out a thick wad of cash. "Looks like it keeps you dry," she said.

"It's kind of hot," I said, sweltering now.

She nodded, counting the pile of change onto the window

sill. "You should try it in here, with a tank of coffee next to you. The rain sucks for business, but at least it's cool."

"I'm from Maine," I said, ridiculously, when what I meant was that I wasn't used to the heat.

"That's in the north, right?"

"On the coast," I said.

"Bet it's nice up there." I could see her breasts, I realized now, underneath her white T-shirt.

I nodded. "Well, it's—different," I said.

She handed me my change. "Don't spend it all in one place," she said with another smile.

"Thanks," I said, shoving it my pocket. Something had happened: The noise and confusion of the city settled inside me, like a flock of birds.

"You just visiting?" she said, looking at me.

"Yeah," I said, surprised at how purposeful it sounded.

"I'll see you around, then," she said.

I smiled back nervously and turned away, the paper bag in my hand. I walked quickly, trying to get out of her line of vision, and as soon as I was around the corner I stopped to get the coffee out of the bag. I took off the lid and took a sip. I was used to having my coffee black, but this was milky and sweet, like dessert.

I wasn't sure which street led back to the institute, but I didn't really mind. I had forgotten to put my hood back up, and the rain fell gently against my skin and on my hair, on the city all around.

13

That night when Walter and Robert didn't come home I found myself cleaning up the newspapers and clearing the sink of cups. I was hungry but not certain if I should go out at night alone. By the time I gave up and went to bed I had resolved to get the stove working again so I could cook my own dinner. In the middle of the night I heard them coming up the stairs, quarreling. It would be several weeks before I learned that the middle of the night was hardly very late for them, and that quarreling was little more than a conversation. I turned over in my bed and listened, though I couldn't make out any of the words, and before I knew it I was asleep again. In the morning they were downstairs again as if nothing unusual had happened, and Walter went merrily off to the university.

Though Robert still seemed intent upon emphasizing how unnecessary my work on the card catalog was, he brought me into the library as soon as I was finished with breakfast to show me how the computer worked.

It was a beautiful room, with three arched, diamond-paned

windows facing the sunny street. Books were packed tight along the other walls, their spines glistening; the bookcases were ingeniously fitted with two rolling ladders that reached the top shelf. I thought of the living room at home, the stepladder always stacked with books, new piles of them growing up around my father's desk like weeds. The ceiling was high as a cathedral's, or felt that way, and when I looked up I saw that it was painted with a delicate map of mythic constellations.

"Just like Grand Central!" Robert said when he saw where I was looking. "And over here we have, as you can see, the entire Loeb classical library, and over here we have, let's see, more classical libraries! And in this section? Books about Rome." He seemed to think it was all a joke. "Oh, and this wall is all Ovid: *Amores, Heroides, Ars Amatoria.* One gazillion editions of *Metamorphoses.*" I wandered over to stare. Some of the books I recognized, of course, but it was hard to believe how my father had managed to leave any of these behind.

"Arthur used to have wonderful parties in here," Robert was saying. "Drove your father crazy."

I smiled blankly, unable to picture my father having anything to do with any party. I wished I hadn't called him the day before with nothing to say but that I had arrived—now I wanted to tell him I'd seen the library. But neither of us were used to the phone. Even when Julie had been interested in calling me he'd kept the ringer turned off, and now that I'd gotten in touch he might just turn it off again.

It turned out the task involved typing information from the cards in the card catalog into tiny boxes on the computer screen called, obscurely, "fields." I didn't tell Robert I hadn't been on a computer before, except for the one in the library at school. The keyboard wasn't any different, anyway, from the typewriter, and I could tell he was impressed at the speed with which I typed in the first card. He didn't say another word about my not bothering with it; he left me to it and told me he'd be in his study if I needed anything. I typed until lunchtime and then went upstairs to change.

Robert emerged just in time to see me coming downstairs in Julie's blue dress. "All dressed up for lunch?" he said, making me regret it instantly.

I waited for Nate on the steps. The weather had cleared up, and the sun was all over the place. I clutched my arms, noticing suddenly how pale my shoulders were, and thought of Julie in her bikini. When Nate came to pick me up he didn't say a word about my dress: We marched rapidly down the block, already late to meet his sister, Liz, who was several more blocks over. She didn't like it when he was late, he explained.

Liz was waiting for us on the corner of Seventh Avenue and Thirteenth Street, digging intently in her handbag, and her hair, which hung in a soft curve in front of her face, flashed with sunlight. The object of her search was a black metal case containing black sunglasses, which she slid on just as we got to her. She was wearing a pearly white button-down shirt that opened at her breast, showing her delicate, richly tanned collarbone. "I've been doing the wedding stuff all day," she said as Nate gave her a kiss.

Nate introduced me, and she nodded, her lenses reflecting the street behind us. "It's really bright, isn't it?" she said.

Before I could answer she was digging in her bag again.

"I thought you quit," Nate said when she got out a pack of cigarettes.

"Not with all this wedding stuff," she said, pulling one out and lighting it. She exhaled prettily. "What are we eating?"

She seemed used to having people watch her smoke, I thought, used to having people watch her do most things. Julie was like that too, but it always seemed to me that Julie was also listening. At least it looked like she was, even if she was thinking about herself. Whenever I drifted off into my own thoughts I tended to look sad, and once in a while someone would ask me what was wrong. I would glance up in surprise and Julie would laugh affectionately, in my defense. "You're so spaced out!" she'd say.

"I don't want to have anything fattening," Liz said, checking her watch. "Have you figured out if there's any good salad around here?"

"She just got here," Nate said, before I realized she was speaking to me.

She paused, I thought, to look over my dress. "Oh, that's right." She smiled. "From Maine, right?"

"We were thinking about falafel," Nate said.

"Thanks. The perfect diet food."

"She's never had it," he said as we moved up the sidewalk. There wasn't room for three of us, and I walked behind, awkward and tall. Nate towered over her, though I guessed, by her offhand cruelty, that she was the older of the two. None of the girls in Yvesport were as small as she was and still so bossy.

People streamed out of the subway exit on Seventh Avenue like ants from a crack, and Nate and his sister walked smoothly around them. I tried to keep up, bumping into passing pedestrians, turning to go sideways between briefcases. They stopped to wait on the corner for a light and a man pulled up next to me on his bike.

For a minute he balanced miraculously on his pedals, his calf muscles braced, sun soaking into his dreadlocked hair. When the bike finally tipped he put his foot out to brace himself against the curb. He saw me looking at him. "Hot," he said, adjusting the canvas strap over his shoulder.

I smiled timidly back at him, glancing over at Nate and his sister for help, but they were too engaged in conversation to notice.

He saw me demur. "But not as hot as you!" he murmured, as if to give me what I asked for.

I looked away, confused.

"Whoooeee!" he crowed as he rode away.

Nate looked up vaguely to see where the noise was coming from, but the man had already taken off, pedaling hard to make the next light. "You knew Dad had to be sailing in June," Nate said to his sister. "I thought Geoffrey was the one who couldn't do July or August."

"It's not Geoffrey's fault."

"That's not what I'm saying." Nate glanced at the unchanged light. "You never even asked Dad if he could do it that last weekend. I don't know what Geoffrey had scheduled but he probably could have changed it. You have to stand up for yourself. It's like with the dress. You wouldn't have to worry about Mom's dress if you just told her you didn't want to look exactly like her."

"I'm not worried about Mom's dress," Liz said. "It fits me perfectly."

A wave of people started across as the light changed, and I waded miserably into them. Nate's sister would never have worn a dress like mine; I should have dressed like her, I thought. I looked like an idiot. Why else had that man whistled at me?

Falafels, it turned out, were sold on the street. We got in a line on the sidewalk behind a cart that was sizzling and smoking with hot food. I stared at Liz's toenails, which were painted blue. Nate smiled at me encouragingly. I thought of the coffee cart and the strange sweet coffee. Another woman wearing a suit got in line behind us; she shifted her skirt under her buttoned jacket and sighed. There were two more people in front of us and one of them was reading a magazine without any pictures, held up close to his face. The man inside the cart was concentrating; he lifted a metal basket out of hot oil and dumped out the falafel like crabs from a trap.

"So how long are you here for?" Liz asked, digging again in her purse. She always seemed to be looking for things.

I shrugged. "A few weeks," I said, not sure whether she was listening.

"At least that means *you're* not going to be moving in with those two queens," she said, looking at Nate.

"It's not like I was really going to do that," Nate replied. "Anyway, it's not like they're contagious."

We were at the head of the line, and Liz gave the man inside the cart an imperious smile and ordered her sandwich without hot sauce. "You don't want hot sauce," she said, touching my arm.

If anyone was a queen, I thought to myself, it was Nate's sister. It was a better name than faggot though, which was what we called them in Yvesport. I always thought it sounded like a bug.

"Queen" was kind of right, for Robert anyway—flighty, regal, dramatic—and for Walter too, in a more matronly way. *Two queens.*

"Hot sauce?" said the man behind the cart, dousing my sandwich with red juice.

"Let's sit in the sun," said Liz, signaling to Nate.

When we'd gotten our sandwiches he led the way toward some park benches, stirring up a group of pigeons on the way. They settled right down again, and came bobbing back toward the woman beside us, who had obviously fed them something from her sandwich. Mr. Blackwell would have waved them away, I thought, though it wouldn't have done much good—they were all over the park we were in, and with people on nearly every bench they had too good a chance for food.

"I'm thinking about getting Mom and Dad to help me buy an apartment, anyway," Nate said casually, as if he hadn't liked the way the last conversation finished.

"So you can pay what's left of the mortgage with your graduate student fellowship and your after-school gig?"

"At least they don't have to pay for my wedding."

I was sitting between them, juggling my messy sandwich, which was burning the sides of my mouth.

"It's not my fault that's the tradition," Liz shot back at him. She looked at me. "If you ever get married, Miranda, you should elope." I nodded, my mouth full. "How's your sandwich?" she asked.

"Delicious," I said.

"You should eat it with the tinfoil on." She held up her sandwich to show how she had folded the foil back. The bottom of mine had leaked all over the lap of my dress. I stood up and batted uselessly at the dark spots of oil, making little pieces of lettuce jump up and down on my skirt to create more spots.

"I always do that," said Nate, giving me a clean napkin. He had already demolished his own sandwich and was using his other napkin to wipe a little bit of hot sauce at the corner of his mouth. He balled up his paper bag and tinfoil and aimed it at a nearby trash can. It landed deep inside and his sister watched with satisfaction. They had the same nose—pert on her, well-defined on him. They had, in fact, girlish and boyish versions of everything: Her fine, graceful shoulders were square and strong on Nate; her narrow waist translated to his long torso; her blue eyes into his handsome green. No doubt, I thought, standing there in my stained skirt, they were perfect children, like Julie and her brother in their Christmas cards, always dressed in the right clothes.

"Fried food's probably good for you," she said to him as she got up, walking over to deposit her trash more delicately. "Slows your big brain down."

Nate stretched his long body, pretending not to hear her. "I was thinking I could show Miranda your gallery before we go back to the institute," he said.

I could feel the stains on my skirt deepen, but Liz looked pleased, and soon we were headed back toward the West Side. She had been working at the gallery for a year, she explained on the way over, but already she hated it. Her boss was a prima donna, she said, and so were all the artists. When we arrived she rang the doorbell and we could see a girl with a short ponytail, wearing a shirt just like Liz's, coming across an empty wood floor to answer the door. I glanced at her nose, thinking maybe they were all related, but it was freckled and sort of broad.

"The tent people called," she said to Nate's sister, holding the door open for us.

"I told you," Liz rolled her eyes. "Did they say they could get the white one?"

"They said to call them back."

"Like they ever answer the phone."

"They sounded nice," the girl said, to be helpful. She, too, was pretty in a polished, shining way, her skin smooth as wax.

The gallery had offices on one side and open space on the other, with glass windows down to the floor that faced the street. There must have been no more than ten paintings on the walls. They were all black and white, shapes made of thickly painted lines.

"Those are Franz Kline," Liz said. "We're about to take this show down."

"Cool," Nate said, walking over to one of the canvases.

I looked at the nearest one: a picture of a structure, like a bridge, the white around it like melting snow. Franz Kline was the artist's name, I realized, peering at a small plaque on the wall: "Franz Kline, oil on canvas, 1953."

Up close the black streaks looked huge and flat, but when I looked around the room they jumped out at me like angry letters. Who would think of these things? I felt very small, standing in front of each one. They were giant and bold, and meant nothing but themselves. Or they meant everything, but nothing specific. Had they been done quickly? Each one took up its own space, balanced. Mr. Blackwell would have waved them away. They were only black lines. For a minute I wanted to scatter them like pigeons.

Nate's sister was talking about the wedding again. I heard Nate walk over to chime in. The paintings stared at me. I stood there in my stained blue dress, looking back, hopelessly innocent. Did everybody already know this? That you could make something like this? I looked back at Nate and his sister, talking by the door. Maybe they'd all seen things like this before.

They looked at me as I approached. "What do you think?" said Nate's sister, coy.

"They're wonderful," I said, unable to stop myself.

She smiled. "They've been really popular," she said.

Popular! I looked back at them, amazed. Maybe everybody knew these things. Maybe *this* is what a city is like. The phone rang and she gave Nate another kiss before she rushed off to get it.

"God—sorry," Nate said, holding the door open for me as we left. "It's hard to get her to talk about anything else, you know? She's been freaked out about the wedding for like a month. They've invited four hundred people."

"Gosh," I said, still thinking about the paintings. People smiled when they passed us, stepping slightly to the side, making more room as if we were a couple. Nate paused for a moment to let a fragile old woman wobble by with her tiny dog on a leash.

"It's mostly for my parents," he said.

"What is?"

"The wedding," he said, looking at me curiously.

"Oh," I said, wondering suddenly if he and Liz had ever disappointed their parents. It seemed impossible. "Were you really thinking of renting that room?" I asked as we neared the institute.

"Not really. I think it would be a little weird, living there and also working there, even if it's only a few days a week. But it's a great deal."

I nodded, relieved.

"So how long was your father at the institute?" he asked.

"I'm not sure," I said. "I think he helped Arthur Mitchell start it, or start the library anyway."

"Sounds like Arthur was a real character," Nate said. "Not that there's any shortage of eccentrics there now."

Two queens, I thought again. Did they think I didn't know?

"So I guess I'll see you tomorrow?"

I looked around, startled to realize we were standing on the corner of the institute's block. "Oh—I guess so," I said.

He gave me another little bow. "Thanks for coming to lunch," he said, before he turned to go.

14

I didn't go back to the coffee cart right away. For the first week or so I walked around the West Village watching what other people did. I found the café that I figured Robert liked to go to, a glassy affair where women perched on stools and read magazines and the boy behind the counter had a nose ring. The music was blaring, and the air-conditioning gave me goose bumps. But the first time I ordered an espresso there, and watched the rich dark rivulet trickle out from the shiny machine into a cup below, I understood exactly why people kept coming. Most people loaded their espresso with mountains of foamy steamed milk, but alone, it was like nothing I had ever tasted—dark yet sweet, rich yet fresh as the steam it was made from. One cup and I was cured of Walter's watery coffee.

Afterward I would sit down at the computer in the library and type the way I did when my father was sober, as if we were both under a spell. I took the drawers out of the big card catalog and set up a system, moving the cards from one drawer to another when I was finished, like pressing the return button on the typewriter. Though the institute was filled, four days a week, with the noisy sounds of the boys who came for tutoring, an espresso left me capable of a kind of focus that could make everything disappear: laughter, running in the hallway, the occasional thunder of Robert or Nate intervening. When Robert was there he always shut the door quietly, with a little nod to me, as if I was playing the piano.

The boys came from private schools around town, the crests of which were sewn onto their school blazers. I wasn't certain whether Robert insisted they keep their uniforms on during his tutorials, but the ease with which they wore their little coats and ties as they pushed and shoved each other in the halls reminded me of the town meetings Mr. Blackwell and my father never went to, with city officials and businessmen from Bangor deciding to tear down houses. My second coffee break, I quickly decided, would be scheduled during the time that the boys came in, so as to avoid the mayhem in the hallway and on the front steps.

The fourth night that Robert and Walter weren't home for dinner I began to clean the kitchen in earnest. I tested the oven to see if it worked and noted the sizes and types of electric burners that needed to be replaced, and then I dug for pots and pans. Before I knew it I was taking all the boxes out of the cabinets: I unearthed several dozen wineglasses, which I washed and turned over on a towel to dry, and I found saucers for all the teacups, which I rinsed and piled on the counter like a long, shiny white snake. I still hadn't found any pots and pans when I opened a box of the same whiskey glasses my father drank from at home. I knew what they were before I unwrapped the first one from its tissue paper: he drank from them every night.

They were made of thick glass, diamonds cut on the outside and a clever triangular pattern on the base that made it difficult to judge the level of the contents from above. They'd seemed almost magical to me when I was a child, like a kind of crystal ball. Once I'd seen my father holding one over his eye, late at night, to look at the way the kitchen kaleidoscoped through the bottom. I had always imagined he saw the kitchen in a star of fragments, the wood floor jig-jagging and the windows and walls turned upside down. But when I held one up to look through it myself the floor of the institute kitchen was only blurry, the grooves in the glass dusty and unimpressive. I put the glass down and looked around at the piles of tissue paper and empty boxes, suddenly realizing what a mess I'd made. The evening had come without my noticing it, and the glasses I had cleaned shone with a dim, watery light. Dusk would be filling the living room at home, and I knew my father would be watching it too, surprised to find himself in the dark.

"Hello?" Someone unlocked the front door of the institute, and suddenly the hall light flashed on. "Miranda?" said Nate, standing in the kitchen door.

"Oh, hi," I said, embarrassed. "I was just—cleaning glasses."

"Whoa. I guess they used to have a lot of parties, huh?"

I looked at all the glasses on the counter, the cups and saucers, realizing he was right. Cocktail parties. No wonder there were no pots and pans.

"Where are Walter and Robert?"

"I'm not sure—they're not usually around for dinner," I said, trying to sound casual.

It turned out Nate hadn't eaten dinner, and we decided to go to a place around the corner, but on the way there I told him I hadn't been on the subway yet, and he decided instead that we should ride a few stops, to a Korean restaurant uptown. He ushered me happily through the subway station, and handed me a token to go through the turnstile after him. We went down stairs to a narrow platform, like a sandbar, between the tracks, and voices crackled incoherently over the speakers. Everyone looked anxious, as if they'd been down there for hours, but a minute later our train came through, blind and clumsy, all its metal cars bumping and screeching behind it. Its sides split open with an uneven chime, and a few people stepped out. We stepped in and as we heaved into motion I grabbed the metal pole beside me. Nate smiled encouragingly.

When we surfaced again from underground, the buildings were tall and lit up, their outsides all windows. Nate headed straight across the street through the traffic and taxis and we walked down another street glowing with Korean signs. Inside the restaurant everybody was speaking in Korean; the waiter led us through the crowd to a table and dropped our menus. The tables were sizzling, and each of them had its own barbecue grill. Next to us a girl with ponytails knotted in bundles above her ears plucked a shrimp from the grill in the middle of her table and popped it into her mouth. The boys across from her said something in her singing language and she laughed.

Nate had to point to the pictures on the menu to show the waiter what we wanted. "So what do you think of New York?" he asked when the waiter was gone, breaking apart his chopsticks.

"I haven't really explored that much," I admitted.

"It must be a pretty big change for you," he said. "Robert

told me you and your father live on an island? Have you ever been to a big city before?"

"Bangor," I said, as if it were nothing. "But not that often." In fact I'd gone there exactly twice, once with Julie and her brother when Mrs. Peabody got a brand-new car, and once with my father and Mr. Blackwell in his truck, when Mr. Blackwell persuaded my father that he needed to buy a new generator. We'd had lunch. I had a milkshake and they had frothy beers at a place with a big television inside.

"I'm not a big-city person," Nate said. "I love the ocean. I think I could probably spend my life at sea."

"But didn't you grow up in the city?"

"Oh, yeah," he said. "But we have a place on Long Island. I used to spend every summer there, on the water. I taught sailing."

I nodded. Even Mr. Blackwell, who'd spent his life on boats, didn't know how to sail. The carrier fleets had been equipped with fuel engines before he was born. The few sailors who undertook the tides of the Bay of Fundy were sailing boats owned either by wealthy summer residents or by whale-watching companies making their money on day cruises. Once in a while I would see a lone yacht approach our shore, its clean white sails fluttering politely before it turned away, like an overdressed dinner guest, too shy to sit.

The waiter returned to cover our table with small white dishes of pickles and sauces and Nate looked them over expertly. "Try that," he said.

I picked up the chopsticks the way he had, improvising, and managed to put a tricky tangle of seaweed into my mouth.

He watched me chew. "Kind of weird, right?" He popped a fishy-looking thing into his mouth without hesitation.

Nate explained that he had also been a rower in college (more evidence for his attraction to water) and afterward he had gone on a trip in the Mediterranean, on a replica of an ancient warship. It had been built to resolve a long-standing controversy about the design used by the Greek and Roman navies. He had studied Latin since he was a boy, but that was how he had become interested in classical history and decided to go to graduate school.

My father always used to lecture me on the difference between myth and legend and history. Myths were "imaginary," legend was "unverifiable," and history was "fact," and anyone who mixed them up, he liked to say, was a sentimental fool. Recreations of Odysseus's journey, fictions of Ovid's exile, or any other flights of imagination which used the ingredients of antiquity for their own purposes made him peevish. I had once found a novel about Ovid's romance with a sorceress in the library, and when I brought it home he said it would be of better use inside the stove.

Evidently someone had published an article about Nate's voyage, which he said he'd show me. He'd gone with a group of rowing friends from college, and a few of them had stayed behind to work on the project, funded by the Greek Ministry of Tourism. "Did you study classics in college?" he asked, noodles in thick red sauce swinging from his chopsticks. "Robert said you were helping your dad with his translation."

"Well, typing it," I said, skipping lightly over the first question. "I didn't really have to understand what he was saying."

He smiled. "Well, you certainly catch on fast with the chopsticks."

I laughed, and he brightened. All he really wanted to do was make me laugh, I thought, as the waiter put our main dishes in front of us. It wasn't much to ask. Both the dishes Nate had ordered involved barbecuing, and he set to work, laying strips of meat and seafood on the grill. It sizzled excitingly.

"It looks delicious," I said, trying to relax.

We drank some beer, and we cooked and ate everything that was given us; by the end of the meal I had begun to lose my grip on the chopsticks, and Nate was getting better at making me smile. "That girl we met at Liz's gallery is having a party next weekend," he said, as the table was cleared. "Liz says it's the last one she'll go to before her wedding."

"When's her wedding?"

"October," he said, rolling his eyes. "You wouldn't believe how much work it takes to plan. There are all these ridiculous rules. Like, there are three different bouquets: one to walk down the aisle with, one to throw to the bridesmaids, and then one to leave the wedding with. She has to pick them all out separately."

"What happens if she just doesn't buy them?"

"She turns into a pumpkin, I guess."

"That doesn't sound so serious," I said, laughing.

"You should come to the party," he said, smiling again.

It was warm and summery when we left, though I hadn't remembered it being that way when we went in, and we decided to walk back downtown. Nate walked as if he were still ushering me, the way he had in the subway and in the restaurant. There was a giddy air of expectancy between us, and when we got to the institute we both paused before the steps. I said goodnight quickly and went up the steps without turning around, but my heart was beating fast as I unlocked the door and let myself in.

Walter was awake in the kitchen, and I went down the hall to say hello. "I'm using the glasses you found," he said, holding up a wineglass with drunken triumph. "And where have you been?"

"With Nate," I said, a little flushed. "We went to a Korean restaurant."

"How terribly unromantic. I hope he was a perfect gentleman in spite of it."

"He invited me to a party next weekend," I said before I knew it.

"Did he? We'll have to get you all dressed up."

"I don't think it's formal or anything," I said, wishing I had kept my mouth shut.

"Not *that* kind of dressed up," he said. "Just—" he glanced at my jeans—"something pretty."

"Well, I won't wear these," I said, starting to feel impatient. He was drunk. I was about to make my escape when we both heard the front door open, and Robert came down the hall. I saw Walter glance at the bottle on the table, as if he was thinking of hiding it.

Robert was wearing a suit and had tossed the jacket over his shoulder; he put it carefully on a chair, taking in the wine, Walter's slumped posture, and the sea of drying glasses. He looked extraordinarily handsome—a cutout model of a man, like my father in the picture with Arthur, I thought suddenly.

"Guess who invited Miranda to a party?" Walter said.

"Someone who doesn't have any glasses?" he said, wandering over to examine them.

"Your beloved Nathaniel," Walter said, watching him. "I think you ought to take Miranda shopping for a new outfit."

"Where did you find all these?"

"Miranda found them. She's cleaned them all."

"I see that," Robert said, picking one up and walking over to the sink to fill it with water.

"Don't you think she needs to buy a New York outfit?"

"I don't mind what she wears, Walter. It's not my business."

"Look who's snippy."

Robert sighed, still standing by the sink with his water. "You're the one who's snippy."

"If you were to judge between the two of us, Miranda, whom would you say was snippier?"

"I would say I'm going to bed," I answered.

Robert raised his glass. "Well said!"

15

After a week or more had passed Robert was not quite as hostile to me as he had been at the start, but he continued to disagree with Walter at every opportunity. No matter how late Walter had been out the night before, he was always cheerful in the morning, and seemed to look forward to pouring me a weak cup of coffee as soon as I came into the kitchen. But as soon as he heard Robert on the stairs he got quieter, as if he was bracing himself. They would greet each other politely, but even as they spoke, they were constantly turning away from each other, furiously giving signals of disregard—reading the paper, getting up from the table just as a joke was being told.

"Is that library project keeping you busy, Miranda?" Walter would say, his manner suddenly stilted, while Robert pretended not to listen. It didn't matter what I answered; I knew Walter was not speaking to me but to him. Not that he expected an answer from Robert either. Both of them were making a show of not needing answers. Robert was most convincing in this regard—

at times I felt certain that he didn't really care, and Walter's glum disappointment would cut through me as keenly as if it were my own.

In a misguided effort to please Robert, I determined to get the kitchen working. It wasn't hard to find a set of pots and pans in one of the discount stores that lined Fourteenth Street, but I had to go to various hardware stores to find the right replacements for the burners and an oven thermometer that I could suspend from the top rack. I had started wearing Julie's dress again, the unstained one, which at least was cool; the sun had been beating down for days, and there wasn't a breath of air to relieve it.

It was in this frame of mind, weary and pleasantly blank, that I finally stopped by the coffee cart for the second time. The woman inside had taken her hat off to fan herself, and her hair underneath was black and shiny. "Bet it doesn't get this hot in Maine," she said, pulling it back on with a tug.

"No," I said, blushing before I knew it. She smiled, knowing she'd caught me off guard, as if it was an old trick.

"Where are *you* from?" I asked, rallying.

"Washington Heights," she said, amused. "But I was born in the Dominican Republic, if that's what you mean. You like it regular?"

"Black, please."

I saw her glancing at my dress before she filled the cup and put it on the sill. "Sixty cents," she said.

I gave her my change and she watched me lift the lid and take a sip.

"You can peel that little tab back you know," she said.

I looked at my cup, not sure what she meant.

"On the lid," she said, pointing, when I still didn't see it, and then suddenly she had stepped out the back and was coming toward me.

"It's made so you can drink it with the lid on," she said, replacing the lid as soon as I handed it over. "And then you just tear this tab back—it's supposed to stick." She pushed at the plastic tab with her forefinger, trying to anchor it.

Up close she was not as tall as I had expected, but more compact, her body thickly set. Her cotton T-shirt smelled sweetly of fabric detergent. "It's supposed to work," she was saying, her brow furrowed, as the tab popped up again, and then I noticed she was blushing too.

"At least now you can drink it without pouring it all over yourself," she said when it finally worked, handing it back, nervous.

"Thanks," I said, looking at her.

"Too bad the coffee sucks," she said, putting her hands in her pockets and backing up a little. "What I need is a good espresso machine."

"Can't you put one in there?"

"Nah," she said, looking through the window at the big metal tank. "You need a generator. That thing runs on propane. Even when you put good coffee in there it tastes like shit—it's just sitting on top of a flame all day." She smiled, calmer. "Bet you're looking forward to that now," she said with a nod at the coffee in my hand.

"I'm not that particular," I lied, looking down at the coffee, wondering why everything we said seemed to matter so much.

But she was looking away already, at a young man coming toward us in green hospital scrubs. He shouted something in Spanish and she laughed, turning to go back into the cart, as if she'd been chastised.

"You can't just stand around talking to all the pretty girls," he said, scolding her prissily in English when he got closer, smiling at me. "There's coffee to make."

"I was telling her why I can't make espresso in here," she said, pouring his coffee as if she was used to him.

He rolled his eyes. "I wish," he said. "You'd have a line around the block."

I excused myself, feeling their eyes at my back as I hurried away with my coffee, wishing I hadn't stayed. For some reason I was sure they were making fun of me, and the feeling only got worse as I got closer to the institute. It turned out that the coffee did in fact taste terrible, and as soon as I got back, I put down my packages and set the machine for a fresh pot.

I cleared away the few newspapers that had accumulated since I'd cleaned up, and decided the stove needed a good clean. I soon discovered that the lid on top of the range had not been opened in years, and it was clear that, aside from the grime, the coils needed to be replaced. I had a few hours until Robert and Nate's classes started and I would have to hide myself in the library—time enough, I decided impulsively, to get the stove working.

I had always prided myself on being able to concentrate with equal intensity upon the various tasks I set myself, or that my father required of me. At home I could split firewood all day until each log broke open with a snap; I could bake a pie with perfect crusts; I could shuck a bucket of clams, all without, for one minute, thinking of anything else. But as I propped open the top of the range like the hood of a car, I kept returning to the woman stepping out of her cart, and that rush of shame as I walked away. Later in the library, I found myself listening in a kind of panic for Nate, hoping he might come in before his classes, and when he didn't, and I heard the voices of boys come and go and the institute got quiet, I started to dread another evening alone. I missed my father. I missed the way it felt to have him in the house. I missed his hunched shoulders, his quiet glances; I missed him knowing, whether he cared or not, that I was there.

The next morning I got up early and made breakfast for Walter and Robert. Walter was ecstatic over the smell of the bacon and sat down happily in front of his omelette and home fries, thrilled that the stove was working, but Robert looked at the clean surfaces with suspicion, and sat down with a scowl.

"I only had to replace the burners," I said to Walter after he expressed his amazement for the third time. "I'm not sure the inside of the oven will work as well."

He looked at me with surprise. "What would you put in there?"

I smiled. "I don't know, a pie?"

"A pie!" He looked over at Robert, trying to coax him into astonishment.

Robert reached for the salt to shake it on his omelette. "You haven't been telling your father what a mess this place is, have you?"

"No," I said.

"Oh, stop it," said Walter.

"Well, I don't want Peter thinking he's got dibs on anything else besides that island of his."

"Don't be childish, dear. His daughter has just made us a fabulous breakfast."

"His daughter is not our housemaid," Robert said, "no matter how convenient it is for *him*."

Walter rolled his eyes. "I don't see anyone else getting up to make breakfast," he said. "And if you're interested in having it again I suggest you be more polite to our guest."

Robert took a swallow of his coffee and picked up his newspaper. For a minute it occurred to me that Robert was like my father, but my father was never angry unless he was drunk, and he had never been angry with me.

"Don't mind him, Miranda, he's just in some mood."

"I'm not in *some mood*."

Walter sighed. "Well. I guess we'll just have to talk amongst ourselves."

I knew it wasn't personal, but it still wasn't nice. I thought as I typed in the library later that my father had never been that mean—but then, he had been, I realized—with Mr. Blackwell. It was a petty kind of meanness, a meanness that was meant not so much to be hurtful as simply to be disrespectful, a meanness—like the night he brought the lobster home—meant only for those who understood exactly how important the hurt really was.

When I got to the coffee cart that afternoon the woman who ran it was throwing empty boxes into the back of her van. She slammed the doors shut and took out a cigarette and lit it, staring absently at the pavement. I thought of the way Mr. Blackwell used to look after a day on the water, his coveralls still on, staring at the clean decks as if the whole day were written there—the sloshing waves, the ropes and hauling chains, the blood and tangled nets.

"You already closed?" I asked.

She looked up and smiled. "I have to go to the garage," she said. "Did you want some coffee?"

"That's okay," I said.

"It's probably pretty nasty by now anyway."

"I was thinking you could put an espresso machine in there," I said, not wanting to walk away. "You could just run it off a generator in the back of your van."

"I've thought of that, actually—but I think the cords would be illegal. You're not allowed to have them just hanging in the street."

"How long would it have to run for?" I asked.

"I get here at five," she said, taking a drag on her cigarette, looking at me.

"And you leave at one—so, eight hours?"

"Yeah."

"Couldn't you just put a small battery-operated one inside the cart and recharge it in the middle of the day?"

"I still don't think it'd be legal," she said, shaking her head. "They fine you for everything. They fine me if I'm not wearing my hat."

"Really?"

"Yeah, they come around with thermometers, and if your milk's not the right temperature, they fine you for that too." She looked down the street, as if to check for them, and then back at me. "Are you in school?" she asked.

"No," I said.

"You already go to college?"

"No."

"Yeah?" She looked at me curiously. "You going to?"

I shrugged. "Are you?"

"I've already done two years in business administration," she said. She smiled wearily. "I guess you just sound like you're in college," she said, as if she was sorry to have brought it up. She stood up, stretching her back in a show of boredom, and then took one last drag on her cigarette and threw the butt into the street. "I should go up to the garage," she said with a sigh.

Neither of us moved. It seemed like something had happened, a kind of halfhearted rejection, and both of us regretted it. She got out another cigarette, and offered one silently to me.

I took one. She smiled and had her lighter out the instant I put it in my mouth. "You don't look like you smoke," she said, watching me inhale.

I coughed a little, but not as badly as I had with Julie. "What do you mean?" I said, wiping my eyes.

She lit hers before she answered. "You just seem nice," she said.

"Nice?" I laughed, coughing again.

"Yeah, like a nice girl."

"How do you know?"

"I can just tell."

"Are you nice?" I said, exhaling.

"Yeah," she smiled, a little sadly, to herself. "I'm not really a *nice girl,* though."

I glanced at her taking another puff of her cigarette, her dark eyes narrowing for a second as she inhaled. She had her other hand in her pocket, and her arm looked thick and muscular. I was suddenly conscious of the shirt I was wearing, a cotton blouse, and my long hair, tied back in a neat braid.

"Sometimes I guess I'm too nice," I said.

"Yeah, that happens," she said, "but sometimes people just expect a lot, and you think you have to give them what they ask for, so it's not really your fault."

"Whose fault is it?"

"Theirs," she said.

"For expecting too much?"

"Sure." She could see that I wasn't convinced. "Lots of people walk around expecting too much. I see it all the time. They walk up and they're in a rush and they act like whatever they're asking for is already theirs. Like, *I'll have a donut.* No please, no thank you." She looked down the street, let out a stream of smoke. "That's why it's good to be nice," she said, turning back to me.

"What's your name?" I said.

"Ana," she said, putting her cigarette in her mouth in order to extend her right hand.

"I'm Miranda," I said.

"Encantada," she said, smiling again.

16

On my way home that afternoon I stopped to look at the buckets of flowers crowding the entrance of the deli on the corner by the institute. They were impossibly bright and magically out of season: tulips and roses, orchids and carnations, dahlias and zinnias. I had managed to encourage a field of lupine on the island, but the perennials I had planted near our porch had never come out in the splash of life and color that I had hoped. Certainly anything I had ever encouraged to grow on the island had always been hatched in a healthy bed of leaves, whereas these flowers, stripped of their surroundings, looked as bright as candy. Even the lilies—white, big, and open—stared audaciously back at me.

Before I knew it I had picked up a dripping bouquet and brought it to the counter inside. The man behind the register tore a huge piece of purple paper from a roll next to him and wrapped it in an enormous paper cone.

"Everything?" he said, as he rang it up.

I nodded piously, as if they were a gift, and carried the flowers back to the institute like a torch.

A few of the students were leaving as I came up the steps.

"Who are those for?" said a tall one with a face round with baby fat.

"None of your business," said Nate from the top of the steps, holding open the door. The boys giggled and rushed off, racing down the sidewalk.

"Did you buy those for Walter and Robert?" Nate asked as he followed me inside.

"They're for my room," I said reluctantly.

"The place looks great," he said, as if I was going around trying to spruce everything up. "I think Robert's afraid you're taking over."

"I know," I said. Suddenly I didn't want to have any more conversations. "I'm just going upstairs," I said.

"See you Saturday?"

"Yeah," I said, trying not to sound too exasperated. "See you Saturday."

Such a performance, my father used to say every time he got back from town. I always used to picture him standing on the dock, the whole town applauding. It was impossible to imagine him in this city, I thought, as I unwrapped the flowers and set them in a glass on the desk. Even with Mr. Blackwell, before it was just the two of us, I could remember nothing but the pleasure of concentration, each of us at our own tasks, in our own quiet rhythms: sketching, homework, the kettle for tea, preparations for dinner.

I sharpened a pencil and first I drew just the starry outlines of the lilies, trying to get the way that the petals worked, coming in and out of space. Gradually the layers of voices and sirens and brakes outside the window began to fade, and I crawled further in, tracing the tiny pink veins under the soft, shining surface. The petals were so firm they seemed almost tropical: Soon I was digging into the centers, until the stamen swelled with definition, making the petals come lapping out at me. They opened in front of me, wide as a magician's gloved hands, their centers ripe with pollen.

My favorite stories, in Ovid's verse, describe metamorphosis as the culmination of a relentless, heedless desire: Salmacis, a yearning lover who is folded eternally into her beloved's embrace; Arachne, whose ambitious designs become her own spider's web; Cyane, the grieving nymph transformed into a pool of her own tears. Too often, though, metamorphosis is only a whim of the gods: Juno turning Io into a cow in her jealousy over Jove, Diana turning the hunter Actaeon into a stag to be chased by his own hounds because he chanced upon her bathing.

I disliked, for instance, the story of Narcissus, the boy who had fallen in love with himself. In Ovid's version it is inseparable from the story of Echo, though in more popular versions it stands on its own. Echo was a talkative nymph, whose only sin was that she made the mistake of trying to distract Juno during one of Jove's dalliances. In her jealous rage, Juno had taken away the nymph's power of speech, but she had not simply turned her into a mute—she had taken from her the power to speak first. Condemned only to repeat what she heard, Echo took to hiding, it was said, in woods and mountain caves, where she grew gaunt with loneliness until, at the even crueler whim of Fate, she laid eyes on Narcissus.

Narcissus was the son of a water god, and was said to be more beautiful than the nymphs themselves. Echo fell madly in love with him, and followed him in silence for days, until at last he turned and looked behind him. *Is anybody here?* he asked. *Here,* she answered, joyfully echoing back. She must have thought herself, in that moment, beautiful again, for she stepped out into the open, and Narcissus saw the wretched, elusive creature she'd become.

He turned away in horror and Echo withered from that day forward, consumed with shame, until only her voice remained. The other nymphs, long sympathetic to her plight, demanded of the gods that Narcissus meet a similar fate, but Narcissus was too beautiful for any to spurn him the way he did Echo. His end was much more gentle: drinking from a pool of the water he was born from, he is said to have seen his reflection and, believing it was another water spirit, fallen in love with himself. Though the water spirit seemed to return his affection exactly, he would not approach, and Narcissus, paralyzed with longing, was riveted to the spot and turned into a flower bearing his name.

I always thought Narcissus, wasting his youth in vanity, had committed a worse crime than Echo, who was only trying to protect another nymph from Juno's wrath. Ovid never says that Echo lies to Juno, only that she distracts her. But in the end it is Echo who is punished, doomed to live the rest of her life in the shadows, while Narcissus becomes a perennial flower, as immortal as springtime.

The next day I woke up early and left the institute before Walter and Robert came down for breakfast. I went by the coffee cart but there was a line and Ana looked busy; I waved at her and went to get an espresso instead, determined to explore. I went down into the subway and asked the token booth clerk how to get to the one museum my father had mentioned. The stations all looked the same, but at the end of each sooty staircase another city waited aboveground. The Upper East Side buildings are stately and upright, the streets are wide and straight. The Metropolitan Museum of Art was set off from Fifth Avenue by a wide set of marble steps, fountains on one side and Central Park spread out like a garden behind it, as far as the eye could see.

Inside it was cool and vast. The shrieks of schoolchildren in front of me echoed harmlessly off the high marble ceilings, fading as I went in one direction and they went in another, like we were venturing across the ice. I went into the Egyptian tomb, and then through what seemed like endless cases of bowls and cups and little stools; finally the room opened again into a gallery of marble statues. It was full of strong men, straining at things, naked men, looking young and dreamy. They were beautiful, the stone as smooth as liquid, impossibly ancient and perfect but somehow enervating. My father, I knew, would be disappointed that I did not like it more. Suddenly it felt like a test, and I wanted nothing more than to simply go outside, where people were on the steps, sitting and lifting their faces to the sun.

I missed him, I suppose, I thought as I left all the miles of paintings upstairs and went back outside. I went down the steps and onto the sidewalk and kept going, until I found an entrance into the park and headed up a path where the trees were more dense. But on the other hand I wished he was gone, gone from my head, and letting me into the museum on my own. Maybe I

just don't like cities, I thought, looking at the dusty undergrowth, the carefully placed rocks. More than once I noticed
someone walking furtively into the thicket. They were doing
something secret—everyone here was busy, full of their secrets.
My father had been busy too, and here I was, wishing I were
somewhere else. Narcissus, at least, had had a kind of focus. He
was beautiful, and had found purpose in that, while the rest of
the nymphs and water spirits could do little more than play and
chase themselves. And what was I, after all, but one of those silly
creatures, waiting for change to take hold?

17

By the time Nate came to pick me up I'd switched my outfit three times. In the end I had decided on Julie's pink dress, now the only one I had that wasn't stained. He was late, he told me, because he was working on a paper that was due on Monday—but the party would only have just started, he said. As we walked through the West Village the sidewalks were teeming with people. Groups of students called to each other across the streets, chatted idly in front of bank machines, made plans. All the way along Eighth Street shuttered gates covered the shop windows, but when we got to the East Village everything was open again, blinking with noise, cluttered with handbags and hats. We turned down one street and then another until we saw a doorstep with a small cluster of people outside the building where the party was, and when we crossed the street they turned to look at us, their eyes flashing with the city lights. "You know what the apartment number is?" one of the women asked Nate humorlessly.

He had it written on a piece of paper, which he got out of his pocket, and read it aloud to her. We waited while she rang the buzzer, and then the intercom crackled unintelligibly and we followed the unfriendly group inside. A woman in a tiny tank top and frosty lipstick took a contemptuous look at my dress.

The noise of the party was leaking out into the hallway above us, and the girl I had seen at the gallery with Liz stuck her head out over the banister. "Sooo—zanne!" she called excitedly. "What took you guys so long?"

"We stopped at Derek's," the girl who'd rung the buzzer called back.

"Well, hurry up," she screeched, "I'm just about to turn on your CD!"

"That's Yvonne," Nate said.

By the time we reached the top the music was blaring. The group ahead of us had melted into the doorway and disappeared into the kitchen. Yvonne was crouched at the stereo, her back to us. Most of the crowd was clustered in the airless kitchen: tall thin women with shining clavicles, men pushing back damp bangs. The women from the doorstep moved purposefully toward a table laid out with chips and salsa. One of them had a tiny ring in her belly button, showing just under her shirt; she dug a chip into the salsa and a loose glop of it fell onto the floor. She touched her friend's shoulder and pointed to it, and they both squealed with helpless laughter.

"Nate, God, how are you?" a wiry brunette said, approaching us with an amazed expression. "I didn't know you knew Yvonne." She had evidently gone to college with Nate, but knew Yvonne strictly from the summer. Nate turned to introduce her to me but I couldn't hear her name.

"We went to college together!" she shouted at me.

I could see Liz beside the sink, holding the hand of a large, bored man with glasses and talking to a woman who was making drinks.

"You want a beer?" Nate asked me, prompting the college friend to look me over again.

"That would be great," I said. As soon as he left the college friend said something inaudible and went into the living room. I watched Liz grab Nate and pull him into the tight group in front of the refrigerator. I thought of Ana, in the cart, and just as I was thinking that no one at the party looked at all nice, Nate turned to point me out, and Liz gave me a little wave.

It didn't take much for things to realign: I was at a party, in New York, and had someone to wave to. She came out of the kitchen with Nate, carrying two massive red cups.

"I hope you didn't want a beer," she said. "I told Nate you had to try Yvonne's cosmos. They're obscenely strong."

I put the massive cup to my lips, and an involuntary shiver ran through me at the harsh smell of the alcohol, not quite masked by the sweet red liquid it was mixed with.

"Geoffrey, come meet Miranda," Liz said, reaching out for the man she'd been leaning against in the kitchen. He had dark sideburns and a large chin, which gave the impression that he was leaning backward.

"Geoffrey Waters," he said.

"Nice to meet you," I said.

"Geoffrey's finishing a novel," Liz said, pulling his arm around her.

"Emphasis on finishing," he said, for no apparent audience. Even as he was being nuzzled up to he managed to keep his expression aloof, as if he was holding a drink he didn't want to spill. "I'm going to go say hi to Stephen," he said.

"He hates talking about his work," Liz confided over her plastic cup when he was gone. "I want him to finish it before the wedding, but I know he never will."

"That's less than a month away, Lizzie," Nate reminded her.

"I know." She let her eyes skim lightly around the room. "It's not impossible, though." She grabbed the arm of another tall man who'd just come in the door. "Woody!" she said, turning away.

"How's your drink?" Nate said.

"Strong," I said.

"I can get you a beer, if you want."

"That's okay," I said, taking another gulp. *He* was nice, I decided, even if no one else was. It felt good to stand beside him—I felt safe. When I looked around the room it seemed that none of the other men would give me the same feeling. They didn't have his obvious kindness, his broad shoulders, his attentive smile. I watched the self-consciously pretty gestures of the girls dancing and I could see they did not feel as safe as I did; they were drawn to each other in small laughing circles, as if for protection.

"Want to go check out the fish tank?" Nate said, close to my ear.

We went over to the tank, which was casting a weird green light over the dancers. Several fish hovered uncertainly in the china castle, at the bottom, as if they were listening to the music. I put my poisonous drink on a nearby chair, and was thinking that all the people standing up looked like the plastic plants, swaying in the tank. I felt like the fish, swimming in sound, and I was getting ready to explain this to Nate when Liz came over to ask why we weren't dancing.

Nate looked at me and must have seen the panic on my face. "We're looking at the fish," he said.

Liz rolled her eyes. "Can you believe I'm getting married?" she shouted, before she left us again, dancing back into the crowd.

"Do you want to go get something to eat?" Nate asked me. "I didn't think this party would be so loud."

It took awhile to get to the door, but the minute we were spat into the hallway we were alone. We went down the stairs together without speaking. I could hear the voices and music filtering down to us, the way, on quiet nights, parties on the mainland used to carry across the water. I got to the door first and pushed it open. The air felt wide.

"You okay?" said Nate, stepping out onto the sidewalk.

"Maybe I'm a little drunk," I said. We were just about at eye level, with him on the step below.

"You're tall," he said.

"So are you," I said, and before he could lean forward and kiss me, I jumped down on the sidewalk too.

We had been at the party longer than I'd thought, and the buildings looked slumped and exhausted as we walked back through the East Village streets. The sidewalks were empty except for two or three men lingering in the bright light of a grocery store on the corner. I felt brave, just walking along.

"That was an okay party," Nate said, slowing down to accommodate my disoriented pace. "I want to take you to my friend Jim's sometime. My sister's friends are a little weird—

Yvonne was into coke for a while, and sometimes I get the feeling she still is. They like to go to clubs."

"Oh," I said, surprised. "Do you like to go to clubs?"

"Sometimes." He looked at me. "I mean like dance clubs, not like the one Robert took you to."

"I know," I said. Down the avenue a long white limo turned the corner and slipped out of sight.

"Do you like to dance?" he said.

"I don't know," I said, telling the truth for once. "Maybe."

He smiled. "We can go out sometime and I'll take you to a club."

"Okay," I said.

He was watching me. "I keep thinking this must be so weird for you, being in such a big city."

"I was born here," I said, suddenly taking heart in the fact. We had turned onto another avenue where there were more cars. Lights were on in the windows and restaurants and delis were open. I felt as if I might even recognize the street.

Nate turned to hold open the door of the diner for me. The cool air-conditioning came rushing out toward us, and he put his hand on my back, as if to guide me into it. It was bright inside and the wash of fluorescent light over the tables and countertops gave the whole place a strange stillness, though it was nearly full. All of the customers seemed to be speaking in murmurs, along the counter and at the booths going back, alone or in cozy groups, hairdos collapsed and makeup unmasked by the bright light. The waitress walked us straight to the back and put down two menus without a word.

"Nothing like a meal in the middle of the night." Nate said, scooting happily into the booth.

The menu was filled with glossy illustrations of hamburgers and fries, pancakes draped with syrup, sundaes with cherries. I unrolled my paper napkin from my fork and knife and put it in my lap.

"Know what you want to eat?" asked Nate.

"Pancakes," I said, thinking how we used to have them as a Sunday treat when Mr. Blackwell stayed over. "And coffee."

Nate got a hamburger. I watched him smile at the waitress as he gave her our order. For a brief moment I wished I were her and she was the one sitting at the table having to admire him and make conversation. She walked away, slipping her order pad into her pocket, and returned with a pot of coffee.

The food came right away. Nate added ketchup to his hamburger and then replaced the bun on top and picked the whole thing up with both hands to take an enormous bite. "I could never be a vegetarian," he said after he put it down, wiping at the ketchup left on his face with his napkin. "You're not a vegetarian, are you?"

"No," I laughed. I had poured all the plastic tubs of syrup onto my pancakes and was just slicing into them. "I just haven't had pancakes in a long time. My father always says he thinks they're too sweet, but we used to have them all the time when I was little." I glanced up at him, thinking that the story didn't make much sense without Mr. Blackwell, who shared my sweet tooth, but he didn't seem to notice. I took a sip of coffee, wondering if there were other pieces of my life I could leave out just as easily.

He seemed to believe I'd gone to college, and there wasn't much point in correcting him. He hadn't asked about my mother, but Robert might have told him about that. I had never liked having to tell people my mother was dead, or having to explain the accident. What difference would it make if I simply left her in my life, had her making pancakes and baking cookies?

He dipped a few french fries into a puddle of ketchup at the edge of his plate. "So I'm curious," he said. "From a totally neutral point of view, what did you think of Geoffrey?"

"Your sister's boyfriend? He seemed—nice."

He laughed, picking up his hamburger again. "No, really."

"I didn't get to talk to him for very long," I said.

"I don't know," he said, taking the last bite of his hamburger. "I've never felt that comfortable with him. I don't think he's ever going to finish that book he's writing."

"Why are they getting married?" I asked.

"Because they're in love, I hope." He smiled at me curiously. "Why else would they get married?"

I shrugged. I thought of Anne Marie Gleason, who'd married Bill Holmes after graduation because she was pregnant; in Greek myth people married for kingdoms and won brides by throwing spears. "People marry for lots of reasons," I said, sounding more sophisticated than I meant to.

"Yeah, well, unfortunately I don't think Liz has any reason to marry Geoffrey besides that one." He sounded a little offended. "I mean he's not poor, but I don't think he's going to make much money being a writer. And anyway, Liz isn't really like that." He took a long sip of his milk shake. "Did your parents split up?"

"My mom died when I was three. I don't really remember

her." It always came out like that, automatic, a series of facts that never changed.

"Wow," he said, "I didn't know that. Did your father ever think about remarrying?"

"I don't think so."

He nodded, as if that confirmed something.

"It's not that I worry about her being in love right *now*," he said thoughtfully. "I'm just sort of worried that she might not stay in love, if he keeps going along like he is. And I feel bad for not telling her. We're pretty close. But she's so caught up in this wedding stuff, she can't really talk about anything else."

"You seem pretty caught up in it too," I said lightly.

He laughed. "Yeah, that's true I guess. Do you want to try a sip of my milk shake?" He handed it over to me. "Sorry I'm being such a motormouth," he said, watching me as I sipped it. "It's nice to get to talk to you. I'm always afraid to interrupt you in the library. And Robert always wants to talk my ear off."

"He's not as fond of me," I said.

"You're not really his type," Nate said, grinning.

I laughed, though that wasn't really what I meant. I didn't need to take things so seriously, I thought, watching him finish off the milk shake. It was still true that he was the kind of boy Julie would have liked; he was honest, and he was kind, and he was more handsome than any boy I'd ever seen in Yvesport.

By the time we left the pancakes had settled my stomach and I felt almost normal. Nate walked me all the way to the institute without asking if I wanted him to. The sky above the buildings had lightened by the time we got to the institute, and I turned around and kissed him.

He tasted like ketchup—sweet—and faintly of onions, a meaty taste. I felt like we might tip over, standing there, and after a while I asked him if he wanted to come upstairs. He cast a shy glance at the institute behind me, but a minute later he was opening the door with his key, as if he were inviting me in, and we were both climbing the stairs in giddy silence.

My drawings were still in a pile on the desk, next to the bouquet of already fading flowers on the table. He sat on the bed with a smile and reached out to take my hand. His hand felt warm. I was standing in front of him and it seemed the air all around him was warm. I put my other hand on his shoulder, to steady myself.

"You're really beautiful," he said gently, touching my face.

When I leaned down again I felt like an expert. His hands moved under my T-shirt and I kept kissing him, happy with his mouth, interested in the rhythm, until we fell back on the bed, tangled, and I stood back up to take off my dress. He watched me, unbuttoning his belt; I heard the change in his pockets as his pants slid off, landing softly on the floor.

18

The next morning the light was blazing through the window so hard it made the sheets glow. I lay in the heat until I could get up the courage to unwrap myself and move cautiously out of the narrow bed. Nate murmured something, his face pressed heavily into the pillow, and then rolled over. I put on the dress I'd worn the night before, watching Nate's sleeping back, careful not to wake him, and went across the hall for a glass of water.

"Where are you going?" he mumbled into his pillow as I creaked open the door.

"Shhhh. I'm just getting a glass of water."

When I came back he rolled over and looked at me. I sat down on the bed and gave him the glass of water like a nurse.

"Why are you all dressed?" he said as soon as he could put the water down, pulling me back on top of him.

I giggled and we wrestled and soon we were serious again, kissing and moving together. What I hadn't known about sex was that it was like playing—soon we were two porpoises, moving over each other, then we were two snakes. When we woke up again the sun had moved out of the window and we were starving. We pulled on our clothes and snuck downstairs and went outside; we ate lunch, and when we were done Nate gave me a kiss on the forehead and went home to his apartment to work on his paper for school.

I walked south through the Village and across Houston Street. The towers of the World Trade Center glittered distantly in the afternoon sun, like two women still in their evening dresses from the night before. I kept walking, till I was wading through the knotted crowds along Canal Street and Chinatown, past shops jammed with telephones and headphones and cameras and CD players, batteries and watches and toys and tiny jade dragons, lacework lanterns and wind chimes and bird cages hanging from every awning. Some streets overflowed with strange fruits and vegetables, leafy greens and sharp-smelling roots pulled out of the other side of the earth; others were wet with melting ice from the piles of fish laid out cleaned and ready to cook. Before I knew it the crowds gave way and Manhattan reared up again, gloomy and municipal.

I kept walking, the dusty afternoon wind stirring my dress. The empty avenue widened and then narrowed until the buildings rose high above me. I came through to a paved park where the sky was lit unmistakably with the ocean. The sun shone in a dull way over the melancholy benches and trees. Two girls skated past in Lycra shorts, stopping up ahead to adjust their Velcro wristbands and plastic skate straps, preening like birds. A crowd gathered by the water to wait for a boat, and I walked up to find that the ground was paved all the way to where the land dropped off, with no shore, as if the whole island was made of cement.

The bay spread out in front of me, sparkling for miles, bridges and tankers gray in the distance. I leaned on the railing to watch a small ferry go by, water frothing merrily around it, a group of tourists sitting on the deck. Ahead of the ferry, heavy and milky green in the sunlight, was the Statue of Liberty, the water like a carpet at her feet. The sight and smell of the sea almost hurt, it was so close and familiar, like the delicious smell of sheets when you are too tired to sleep; it was already September and I could picture the bay in front of our house, the islands just beginning to color, rafts of eiders by the shore, eagles and ospreys on the hunt, readying to leave for warmer coasts.

I smiled again at the thought of my father remarrying, though I couldn't say why it amused me so much. It was impossible to imagine him applying himself to courtship, straightening his hunched shoulders and putting on a new shirt. Nate seemed to take his not remarrying as a sign that he had loved my mother, but in fact I had never actually thought about him being in love at all. But then he had been here, in this city, and that was hard enough to imagine too: Arthur's parties, the club, his glittering library. As I turned around to look at the buildings, rising away from me as if they spanned as far as the sea, it occurred to me that beyond a doubt my father had loved this island more than our own.

He had never said—the way Mr. Blackwell always did—that the summer was worth waiting for, or that he'd never seen the bay so beautiful. In all the time he'd lived there, he'd never managed to predict the weather, catch a shift from northeast to northwest, or tell when the fish were in and the bay was frothing with krill. When Mr. Blackwell looked out at the bay he saw boats he knew and a map of lobster pots; he saw new heron nests and the stir of cod. But when my father looked out at the sea he looked into the past.

He had been in New York, after all, for nearly as many years as I had been on the island. He'd come here from Boston, where he'd had his only stint teaching in a university. Now I remembered how he'd said he had given up his job to live here; he'd come to the city without a plan. And somewhere out of it he'd met Arthur, by chance, and things had fallen into place. He had stayed, and then met my mother.

I went home along the West Side, past a series of big glassy buildings and a small park, up alongside crumbling old docks and next to a highway. I crossed the street when the buildings got smaller and less factory-like, and before I knew it I was in the Village again, in a neighborhood like the one the institute was in, tiny curved streets and quaint apartment houses. I had always imagined—since all I knew about Arthur was that my father had helped him found the institute—that the picture my father had on his desk had been taken the day the library officially opened. But in fact it could have been taken any day—on their way out to the club, or on their way out for a walk, Arthur holding his cane off the ground, dressed in a dapper suit and ready to explore the bars, the restaurants, the cafés with their little patios, the antique shops and used bookstores.

And as amazing as it seems to me now, though I crossed Christopher Street on that day and did not fail to notice how many storefronts sold condoms and fetish clothing, T-shirts and rainbow flags, it was the antique shops, filled with their friendly miscellaneous clutter, that once more delivered me the word *fag-*

got. This was because I knew one man, in Lubec, whom everybody called a faggot; he owned an antique store and he wore a handkerchief around his neck like a cravat. There were a lot of men here, walking in pairs, and these men, it finally dawned on me, were also faggots—or queens, as Liz called them. The neighborhood was full of them. I simply recognized it the way a few blocks later, I recognized the street I was on, and kept walking. Not once did I think: Arthur was a faggot! Not once did I think that my father might actually have been in love sometime, anytime in his life, with anyone but me.

the age of iron

19

I slept at Nate's apartment for the next few weeks, and the arrangement suited everyone. I came back to type in the library in the afternoon, and sometimes went up to my room to draw if Nate had something else to do. When I peered into the kitchen after the first few days I'd been gone, the toaster was back on the stove and a pile of newspapers, albeit a neat one, was already growing in the corner. The audacity with which I had established myself in Robert and Walter's life startled me; in a matter of weeks all my righteous domesticity seemed to have dissolved along with my nervous solitude.

Nate and I went out to dinner, we watched television, we listened to music. He bought me two miniskirts to show off my legs and we went to movies and bars and parks all over the city. He was still teaching at the institute, which meant he had to write lesson plans, and he was also in school, which meant he had to study. When my father sat down to work it swallowed him whole: his lamp, his chair, the books he liked to keep in stacks on the floor, the piles of manuscript around him—they all became a part of him. But when Nate sat down to work he looked as if he were planning a meal. He would scoot in his chair, arrange his pencils, turn on his computer, get up for a glass of water, sit back down and look at everything all over again. All I had to do was meet his eye and he would walk over to kiss me.

In the first week I was there he showed me the article in his college alumni magazine about his rowing trip, titled "Following a Hero." It began with a photo of the ship, a reconstruction of an ancient trireme, the type Jason of the Argonauts was said to have sailed.

"I was right there," Nate said, pointing at a photograph of the ship, dwarfed by the background panorama of the Mediterranean coast. "That's my oar."

In another photo all the rowers stood on a dock beside the ship. They were muscled and sweaty, a few of them raising their arms to the camera in a victory salute, some with gloves on, some with their hands taped. Nate stood in the back, jostling two other boys who were trying to get up on a pylon that would raise them above the group.

"That's me," he said, as if I might not recognize him.

"So you actually had to row?"

"Some of the time we were sailing," he admitted, turning the page to show the ship under sail. The glossy Mediterranean underneath made it look like a toy. Another section of the article showed the vase paintings, coins, and sculptures on which they had based the design of the ship. The distinctions between myth and legend and history seemed a silly thing to take offense at after all, I thought—why did one have any more claim to truth than another? I leafed through the rest of the magazine, drawn in by Nate's obvious pride. One alumnus was a scientist, who was responsible for the successful regulation of a new pesticide; another owned a cattle ranch, and stood against a fence beside a group of distracted cows.

"My dad knows that guy," Nate said, when I paused to look at the man standing with his feet out of the mud. "He's loaded."

Though he wouldn't have said so, it appeared that Nate was "loaded" as well; he showed me photographs of his house on the shore of Connecticut, which looked like a hotel, and the boat his father raced in Bermuda every year. "Do you think I look like my mother or my father?" he asked as we gazed at a picture of his family together, standing by the net of a tennis court.

"I don't know," I said, looking uncertainly at their perfect features.

"My mother thinks I look more like her side of the family. We all have this pointy nose."

"I think you have a fine nose," I said, turning away from the picture with relief. I kissed the tip of it.

"I didn't say there was anything wrong with it," he said. I kissed him more urgently and when he rolled his eyes I grinned at him, unbuttoned his pants, and took his penis from the tent of his boxers. I was bending over when he pulled me back up to eye level, kissed me, and then led me to the bed.

It seemed to me I had changed. I was Galatea, the statue turned to flesh in her creator's hands. I had come from my island in Maine in my foul-weather gear, typing and cleaning and drawing in my room, and Nate had brought me gifts and made me warm to the touch, a girl in the city like any other. But then when I walked him to class at the university, and watched as he disappeared easily into the throng of students outside the buildings surrounding Washington Square, I would look at the girls with their books pressed to their chests, laughing, talking, walking in short skirts and long pants, high boots and little sandals—and wonder why, in the end, I was still not like them.

The coffee cart was not on my route to the institute when I was staying at Nate's, and there was a café on the corner that he introduced me to. They had a menu of espresso drinks served with piles of frothy milk in various flavors; they had iced drinks and they had a maple scone—Nate's favorite. But one day when he told me he was craving a donut I led him off to Ana's cart.

It was his city, and it wasn't often that I led him somewhere, so even though it was several blocks out of the way, he indulged it like a game. We'd developed a rating system for the restaurants he took me to. When he'd asked me what I had thought of the Korean restaurant he'd taken me to on what we now referred to as our first date, I'd said it was "weird," and he'd pretended to be hurt; thereafter restaurants were termed "good weird," "bad weird," and "plain weird." As I learned to take into account the décor—the fountains in sushi restaurants, the piñatas in Mexican ones—we rated that on the weird scale too.

"Looks plain weird," he said as soon as I pointed out Ana's cart from down the block.

"Wait 'til you see," I said, undaunted, skipping along beside him.

It was morning, and there was a short line of hospital workers and businessmen. Ana's expression was blank and meditative.

As more people got in line behind us I began to wonder if it might be better to come back later—she hadn't seen us yet—but Nate told me cheerfully that the line was moving quickly.

"I'm not getting coffee," he said, peering over the shoulder of the man in front of him to check out the selection of donuts. "Which is the best donut?"

I looked anxiously at the shelves of mediocre pastries, sitting on their greasy strips of waxed paper, already knowing what Nate would think of them. Ana saw me and smiled.

"Hey, Chica," she said, as she turned to pour another coffee. "Been a while."

"I know," I said, as her eyes slid over to Nate. "I told you you need an espresso machine." We were at the head of the line, both of us standing at her window.

"Regular?" she said, with a slightly impatient smile, turning to make the coffee before I could reply. "Just one or you need two?"

"Just one," said Nate, "and a donut. Which one should I get?" he asked me.

She put the coffee down on the counter and for a second her eyes met mine. *Chocolate's a tiny bit crispier,* I heard her saying, the first time I'd met her. I couldn't answer him; I saw her eyes harden as she looked away.

"The lady needs to make her choice," she finally said, giving Nate her customer smile, and leaning forward on her strong arms, "or I'm going to charge double for my time."

He laughed. "You better give me chocolate then," said Nate.

"Good choice," she said without looking at me, turning to pluck a piece of wax paper from the box on the window shelf.

Nate paid and we walked away. I pressed the tab back the way she had shown me and took a sip of the terrible coffee. Nate bit into his donut. "Plain weird," he said, "and plain bad too. How's the coffee?"

"Okay," I said, suddenly sickened by our stupid game. "Anyway, it was only sixty cents."

He aimed his donut for the trash can. "Wanna get breakfast?" he said.

"No," I said, for what felt like the first time in weeks. "I should probably really get to work."

"Does Robert even know what you're doing in there?"

"He seems to," I said. "I think I can probably get it done in a couple of weeks."

Nate didn't respond and we were both quiet. We hadn't talked about when I might go back to Maine, or what would happen when I did. We parted ways at the corner of Seventh Avenue and Charles Street, and he gave me a chaste kiss on the cheek, as if he'd been reprimanded.

There was something hideous, I thought that afternoon at the institute, about Galatea's marble insides turning to flesh, to seething intestines and a squishy liver, inflating lungs and a pumping heart. The tales in *Metamorphoses* rarely ended happily; the process of transformation, of hands turning into claws and feathers sprouting on shoulders, was sometimes a punishment, and sometimes a reprieve. But mostly it was a compromise of some sort, a way to negotiate the chasm between desire and mortality, between human nature and human need.

Galatea had in fact given birth. The progeny of the statue and her creator was Paphos, "upon whose fertile land myrrh grows alongside cinnamon and balsam," and her grandson was the unfortunate Cinyras, whose daughter Myrrha had tragically betrayed him. It was a story I remembered well: Myrrha had had a throng of suitors vying for her hand, and was said to have been very beautiful. But when she was young, her father, Cinyras, who was a king, had allowed her to climb onto his lap while he sat on the throne. She had curled against his chest and she had looked out on the court while listening to his heart; she had seen the world through his eyes and fallen under his spell. She wanted nothing else than to be with him—to share his world and his heart as lovers do.

She could not change her heart. She attempted suicide but was rescued by her loyal nurse, who begged to know what ailed her. When at last Myrrha told her the truth, her old nurse could think of no cure but fulfillment. As soon as the queen was away for a harvest festival, the nurse told the king that a girl in the kingdom was madly in love with him, and had offered to take the queen's place in his bed if he consented to be blindfolded, so as to save her reputation. The king agreed readily enough, but as the nights with his young seductress wore on, he became more and more intent to know her identity. The moment he took off his blindfold and laid eyes on his daughter he went mad with rage, and chased her from his bed with his sword. She fled, wandering across the earth, begging the gods to relieve her of her life; finally they took pity on her and turned her to a myrrh tree, whose bark still oozes with her tears.

I was supposed to be typing but instead I got up and went upstairs to my room. The last bouquet of lilies I had bought for drawing were wilted and hanging their heads, the petals ready to drop. The water in the vase was gone; they had begun to curl back thirstily, the ridges on their surfaces nearly transparent from their will to expand. I touched one with my finger and it dropped to the desk, the missing petal ruining the symmetry.

"Nature has no dignity," my father had said once, when I'd shown him our rose hips, crowded with the shining black backs of thousands of beetles. Even as we watched they plunged their greedy heads into fresh petals, piled lustily upon each other to multiply.

I got out my sketchbook and began to draw the flower with the missing petal. Julie had taught me how to pluck petals from a daisy to see whether or not a boy loved you. "You have to picture someone," she would say, looking at me as if she knew it was the kind of game I might not play right. I drew the flower, and then the stem, lazily following the next stem up to the next dying flower, already losing interest.

After the old nurse saved Myrrha from her suicide, she knew Myrrha was sick with love, but at first she could not guess with whom. Myrrha could not say it outright, and it was not until she managed to moan "my mother is so lucky to have such a man for her husband" that the nurse understood. I had never felt my mother was lucky to have my father for a husband; I'd often wondered if he'd ever even loved her. He had a picture in his bedroom of the day they got married, standing in front of the Municipal Building in New York. A businessman on his way to work in a suit is just entering the frame behind them. My father looks like a paper doll in his tuxedo, as if he'd been pasted in. My mother is holding my father's stiff arm, wearing a winter coat over her pale dress. Nothing indicates that the weather is not warm; the man entering the frame wears his jacket open, and the front of the building is full of sunlight. She seems, even then, as if she might walk into the fog and never come back.

"Why is she wearing that coat?" I'd asked my father once, and he'd picked up the picture to look at it more closely, as if he had no idea what I was talking about.

I had never blamed my father for not loving her, but she must have known it herself. Whether or not her death was an accident it had always been a consolation that he loved me more than he ever loved her. He would not have let me go.

I got into my bed in my strange room with the dead flowers and curled up with my pillow. *He loves me,* I told myself, over and over again, as if I couldn't picture him, alone in our house, moving from the kitchen to his desk, perfectly glad to have me gone.

20

Walter came into the library the next day with a letter from my father. I recognized the stationery the minute I saw the envelope, and when he handed it to me I couldn't resist looking at it, reading my name in my father's handwriting, "Institute for Classical Studies" written with pride.

"How's the little lovebird?" Walter said. "Robert says Nate's been showing you all around the city." I had forgotten it was Sunday, and Walter was at home. "Have you been to any museums?" he asked.

"Not really," I said, shy.

"Your father will kill us if we don't get you to the Metropolitan. Totally worshipped the place, as far as I remember. And you ought to go to the Modern, which he might not approve of. I'm surprised Nate hasn't taken you there. Doesn't his sister work at a gallery?"

I wanted to read the letter but I nodded as he went on about the exhibition there, and even asked him a few questions. When he finally left me alone I opened the letter immediately. It was written on one thick, starchy piece of notepaper, folded in half to fit the small square envelope.

Dear Miranda,
I hope you are well and enjoying the city. I must confess that I am unable to find my favorite pen—the green Parker—and wonder if you might have it. The nib happens to be one that, despite heavy use, still makes a thin, clean stroke.

If you do have it, I hope you will use it to write to your dear father. But please do let me know, in any case, so that I don't have to keep looking under the couch, and all around.
                                        Your father, Peter

I read it over a few times—it was written in his large scrawl, and the two small paragraphs took up the entire page. He'd given me a pen for every one of my birthdays, and I had brought them only because I kept them in a box with the charcoal and erasers and soft pencils I used for drawing. I had forgotten how rare it was that my father ever did anything I didn't expect—in fact he was always losing his pen, and inevitably he had left it in the kitchen, while he was making tea, or it had fallen between the couch cushions, where he'd fallen asleep.

I slid the letter back into its envelope and looked calmly around the library, sensing how nothing had changed. He was home and I was here. I turned over the envelope to read my name again in his handwriting and smiled. I didn't have his pen, and he knew it—he wanted a letter from me.

I went outside. It was a beautiful day, with a hint of fall already brightening the air, and everyone on the street walked with their heads up, as if they were drinking it in. Ana wouldn't be working on a Sunday; Nate, I knew, might be wondering where I was. *Please do let me know, in any case, so that I don't have to keep looking under the couch, and all around.* I got an espresso from the boy with the nose ring, and after a while I took the subway up to the Museum of Modern Art, just for the sake of going somewhere. It was in midtown, near the row of swanky department stores on Fifth Avenue.

The entrance to the museum was a wall of revolving doors, and as I stepped inside one of them there was a whoosh and then the screeching and scraping of the city stopped. There were no noisy groups of school children; even at the ticket booth museum-goers waited in mild-mannered lines. Everyone stood perfectly still on the escalator up to the exhibits, looking out the window at a large walled garden or at the perfectly still people riding down. No one asked for my ticket at the entrance to the Mondrian exhibit, but everyone stopped outside anyway, dutifully reading a dense text on the wall about the artist beside a photograph of him standing on a ladder in a laboratory coat, looking more like a scientist than a painter.

As I wandered in to look at the withered still lifes and heavy landscapes I wondered if I should have come. People moved around the room in trancelike states, as if they'd forgotten about the city outside, the urgent traffic jams, the crowded restaurants, the clickety-clacking of their ladylike shoes. I felt out of place, the way I did in churches, or theaters, as if I didn't know the rules. I stood in front of a messy blue vase with three heavy blossoms, trying to see it for what it was, and nearly gave up. But when I dragged myself into the next room the paintings changed.

The muted colors became blurred and mixed; a network of black lines was all that was left of the trees from the room before. I leaned close to look at a title the way the man in front of me had done. *Flowering Trees,* it said. I stepped back and looked at the lines, the pinkish and bluish gray that filled them, and something dropped inside me, for there was the sky, and the apple-like blossoms. As I looked around the room at the other paintings I saw at once how this man had reorganized things. Brown, black, grays, and pinks intersected: *Paris, 1917,* said another painting, and there it was—a city absolutely, with windows and spires and walls, all troubled, all layered and exact.

In the next room the gray vanished, and the canvases were gridded into black horizontal and vertical lines with red, blue, and yellow blocks of color. Sometimes a color—red, for instance—took up almost the whole canvas, and sometimes there were only black lines, moving and squaring off in different ways, making spaces of their own. Red, blues, and yellows blinked along the black lines in busy little trains. Each canvas was full of excitement but calibrated and complete, ending like a song—just when I was ready to move on to the next.

I wandered dizzily back toward the first room, ready to do it all over again, starting with the trees. I used to have trouble drawing the way branches went up into the sky; I remembered my endless doodling in school, thinking it was impossible to make the branches look as thin as they did in real life, tapered but substantial. But he had done it all at once: the sky coming forward through the trees until the branches seemed like fault lines in the gray-blue. Everything had begun to divide out of its simplest self. The lines had straightened and the panes of sky squared until they were primary, the tree and the sky gone.

By the last room straight black lines limned clean white canvases, balancing the colors of geometry. I looked at the other people, stopping at each canvas, looking at nothing but colors and lines. No one seemed to mind. In the place where tree and sky had shifted, only the elements were left—the lines without design, the colors without context. I thought of my careful record of each lily in my sketch pad; I thought of my whole careful life.

What was I afraid of losing, anyway? There was no regret, nothing but hope in the obstinate boxes of color. It seemed easy, all of a sudden, to change everything. I was in a city, where people felt all this made sense. I could do anything I wanted. I walked against the flow of murmuring people, back to the room with the still lifes. Even then, of course, he had taken liberties. You could see the thick lines of paint, the places where the brush had spread, the color chosen despite the flower.

My father, I thought, looking around again at the booming color in the last room, hated to lose things. He kept each draft I typed, even when only a line or two had changed, and piled them like a snowbank against the living room windows; he had his favorite sweaters, with the patches one on top of another; he had his favorite whiskey glass he rinsed each night. I'd always tried to help him keep things the way they were. After I'd lost his watch, I'd looked for it for years in the rocks at the edge of the cove. I imagined so many times the way it would look when I finally found it—the band eaten away, the face all rusted and still, the minute hand thin as an eyelash—that sometimes it seemed as if I had. I could almost believe we'd put it on a bed of clean cotton, in its own special box.

But there was one thing he'd let go. Though I'd heard him say to Mr. Blackwell that he had "lost interest" in the priesthood, and that he had "lost touch" with his sister, I had never heard him say, the way other people did when politely describing our situation, that he had "lost" my mother when I was young. She'd passed away. He'd simply let her go, like the tree and the sky in the canvas, to build the life he had meant to, of pens and whiskey glasses and books, of solitude and sorrow and contentment.

I walked downtown through the noise, past the blocky buildings, the tall glassy ones, the blinking lights and moving signs on Forty-second Street. I went back to the institute to watch the sky darken from my little room, the windows of the city light up, yellow, red, a grid of constellations—busy, alive, and all my own.

21

The next day I put on Julie's dress and waited until Ana was about to close the cart. When I got to her she was throwing her empty boxes into her van. I saw her glance at me, though she didn't say hello.

"Do you have any coffee left?" I asked.

"I'm packing up," she said, turning a cooler of half-melted ice onto the street. We watched it funnel into a drain by the sidewalk. "How much do you want it?" she said, getting out a cigarette.

"What?"

"The coffee."

"Oh," I laughed nervously. "I guess you've probably gotten to the bottom of the tank anyway."

"Probably," she said, looking at me.

I put my hands into the pocket of my dress. "I was just—I was just wondering what you're doing after this."

She blew out a stream of smoke. "I'm going to the garage to drop off my cart," she said. "Shouldn't you be hanging out with your boyfriend?"

"No," I said.

"You're supposed to say he's not my boyfriend," she said, smiling a little.

"He's not, really," I stammered, vaguely telling myself it meant something that I hadn't seen him for two days. He might even have been wondering where I was.

She laughed, slamming the van doors shut. I watched her bend over to pick up the front of the cart by its trailer hitch and place it deftly on the van's ball mount. "I can take you to a place where you can try café con leche," she said, taking the cigarette out of her mouth to hold it again. "But we have to drop off the cart first."

"Okay," I said.

The passenger seat was set up high and I felt like a child as I climbed up in my dress. It smelled deeply of cigarettes and stale cardboard. She walked slowly around the front of the van and got in, taking the cardboard COFFEE VENDOR sign off the dashboard. The radio exploded into a loud, jangly rhythm as soon as she turned the key in the ignition, and she switched it off.

The silence was terrible. I realized I'd had no idea what we would talk about, or where she might take me. She rolled down her window and moved out into the traffic. It was like coming away from a dock. She was looking at the traffic on both sides of her, her cigarette hand out the window. I rolled down my window too, and was glad for the wind rushing at me. I put out my hand to feel the cool air. "It's like being in a boat," I said, out loud.

"I've never been in a boat," she said, "even though I grew up on an island."

"I live on an island," I said. "We don't have a car."

"Doesn't your island have roads?"

"It's mostly just rocks and trees. And our house. And a cove."

She glanced at me. "And you live there with your family?"

"Just me and my father."

She rolled her eyes. "I think I'd kill my father if I had to live on a pile of rocks with him."

"We're sort of used to it."

"You lived there all your life?" she asked.

"Yeah," I said. It was a relief to be talking again.

I held up her pack of cigarettes and she gave me an amused nod. As soon as I had one between my lips, she was holding her lighter for me, watching me inhale between glances at the traffic. There was an irony to these moments of sudden chivalry—I found them irresistible, and she knew it. She gave me a triumphant look.

"How long have you lived in New York?" I asked.

"We came over from Santo Domingo with my mom when we were kids," she said. "I guess I was seven. My sister was ten."

I nodded, thinking of how often people in Yvesport used to ask me the same question. They always wanted to know exactly when we had become relevant to them, as if they could dismiss any experience beyond the town line. "I was actually born in New York," I said. "But my father took me to Maine when I was two. People used to remind me of it all the time in Yvesport, but now that I'm here, of course, it doesn't matter at all."

She nodded, as if she had understood what I had been thinking. It was difficult to imagine anyone really feeling like they belonged here, anyway; looking out at the street, at the taxis and the trucks, the shoppers and bystanders, and the workers drilling holes into the pavement, it seemed clear to me that everybody was from somewhere else. "Do you miss it?" I asked her.

"The Dominican Republic? Not really. I've been back a few times. My father still lives there." She was quiet for a minute. "Did your father stay in Maine?"

"Yeah," I said. "I'm just visiting."

"You miss it?"

"Not really," I said, smiling. "I've only been here about a month, though," I added, to be fair.

"You seem to make friends pretty quick," she said, as she pulled off the highway onto the exit ramp.

We parked across from open garage doors, and I could see the empty carts inside, some already parked haphazardly for the night, some being hosed down by the men who'd been working in them all day. People were milling around outside; a few men stood and watched the activity as if they owned it. I heard Ana unhooking the cart and as soon as I saw her tugging it toward the entrance I got out to help her.

Though none of the men seemed to notice Ana when she was moving the cart alone, they all noticed me, and one or two even straightened up to have a long stare. A few of them were speaking in another language, but the ones staring at me didn't say a word. I knew she would have preferred that I stay in the van, but the cart was heavy and awkward and I could tell she was struggling. We rolled it in next to a huge Dumpster, overflowing with uneaten donuts and bagels. A few men were shoving their carts around to get space next to a wall hung with hoses; a dark puddle of coffee had pooled over the drain and covered most of the garage floor. Ana unloaded her tanks and dumped them into the puddle. I knew if I asked what to do she would send me back to the van, so I walked over to the hoses to wait for the one nearest to her cart to come free. The man using it scowled at me, and when he was done he dropped it into the puddle and walked away.

I braced myself and leaned over to retrieve it out of the warm brown water, holding it away from my dress to bring it over to her.

"Hey Ana!" one of the men called from across the garage. "How about your friend help me?"

When she turned and saw me carrying the dripping hose I smiled at her apologetically. She smiled back, but there was a wary look in her eyes, as if she was used to this kind of teasing, and I felt a rush of protectiveness toward her. "You better wait in the car," she said.

I watched from the passenger seat as she cleaned the rest of the cart and dragged it into a parking space. I was used to walking onto a dock full of men, but then I suppose I'd always more or less had Mr. Blackwell on my side. I watched her move between them to wash her hands, her shoulders hunched, making herself invisible. One of them said something to her, and they seemed to be joking for a minute; she called goodbye cheerfully as she turned to come back out to the van.

She looked relieved when she got back inside, and neither of us spoke until we were clear of the garage. She offered me a cigarette and the ritual with the lighter restored our confidence. She turned on the radio. *"Bachata,"* she said, grinning at me, moving her head to catch three beats she must have known were coming.

I laughed.

"Next stop, café con leche," she said, thrumming on the steering wheel as we came out on the avenue.

The restaurant we went to wasn't far from the garage. It had a yellow awning painted with the words RESTAURANT CARIBE and underneath, POLLO, CARNE, PESCADO. We got a parking space right nearby and she pulled the door open for me with a hint of pride. It was a tiny little place, with just space enough to walk between the stools at the counter and the back wall. The smell of garlic and meat hung in the air, and somewhere in the back was the slow clamor of dishes being washed. It was mid-afternoon, just before the dinner hour, and there were only a few seated customers. Ana greeted one of the women behind the counter as we sat down, and she came over to give Ana a kiss. When her pretty smile faded I thought she looked beautiful. She had wide, intelligent eyes, accentuated by the way she had smoothed her long kinky hair back into a ponytail. I felt her giving me a second look before she went off to make our coffee.

"Maria's always trying to get me to give up the cart and work here," Ana said as she walked away. "I like having my own thing, though. And the rent's crazy," she added, as if she was still trying to persuade herself.

"It's nice," I said, looking around and realizing it was true. Though it was small, every inch of the space had been put to efficient use. Maria and the other woman had just enough room to move past the hot trays of food and neatly stacked containers, the coffee machines and juice strainers, but it was clean and busy and bright. "I should work here."

She looked at me with surprise. "You looking for a job?"

"Well, no," I said, embarrassed. "I work—in the library of the place where I live. But it's just—sort of isolated." Suddenly I wished I hadn't brought it up. What sort of complaint was that? I thought of her heavy cart, the filthy garage. I thought of those boys in their blazers, quieting as I went past.

"I would never be able to do my job if I didn't talk to so many different people," she said. "I know those guys are assholes, but I don't have to really deal with them. And mostly they're pretty cool with me." She shifted huskily in her chair, as if she was still toughing out that moment. "I mean you can live here and never learn to speak English, or you can just do your own thing." She gave me a brave smile, and suddenly it occurred to me that she was lonely too.

"I think I'm going to be in big trouble if you don't like this," Maria said, setting two frothy cups down in front of us. "But so will you, I think," she added, with a teasing glance at me, "so I'm not that worried."

I took a sip, pretending not to notice Ana's blush. One minute she was all bravado and the next she was blushing. The coffee was delicious, the milk steamed just enough to bring out the taste without getting airy, and the coffee underneath strong and rich.

Maria smiled. "I think she likes it," she said to Ana in English, before she turned away again to take care of a new customer.

"She's from Santo Domingo too," Ana said. "But she didn't come here until she was twenty. She was married."

I nodded, not sure why that surprised me.

"Did you say your parents were divorced?"

"No," I said. "My mother died when I was three. I don't think she was very happy," I added, without really thinking about it.

"How do you know?" Ana said.

"I don't, really," I said, still idly watching Maria, who was reaching for the phone with one hand and lifting a precariously stacked plate off the counter with the other. "I don't know anything about her, actually. But I think I would remember her better if she had been happier. You know? And she looks kind of sad in the pictures."

Ana looked at me. "How old was she when she died?"

I shrugged. "She was married to my father for only a few years."

"Was she pregnant when she married him?"

I blinked. "I guess so," I said, suddenly realizing what the coat in the wedding picture was for.

"Maybe she never wanted to get married or—whatever—have a kid. A lot of people feel like they don't have a choice, and then they kind of hate it. I mean, not that she hated you, or your dad, or whatever. But I mean—it's a reason to be sad, if she was. My sister got pregnant a few years ago and of course the guy left her, but the truth is she never wanted a kid. She was more bitchy than sad and now of course she has another, but that's another story. Women have to do what other people want all the time.

"Maria's husband was an asshole and she had to leave her kid with his family when she came here," she said, nodding at Maria, who was making another customer laugh. "But now she's—I mean she has a whole life."

I looked at Maria, who looked every bit like she had a whole life. "People gave her a hard time for leaving her kid behind," Ana was saying, "but I feel like it's kind of—I don't know—brave. Not that your mother left you behind," she said, turning to me. "I mean, it's just that some women don't really feel like they have a choice, I guess." She took a sip of her coffee, embarrassed.

In fact my mother *had* left me behind, I wanted to tell her, but I couldn't think what made me so sure. Maybe it was just that I had learned to drive through the fog when I was twelve; maybe it was just that I never really blamed her, anyway.

We were quiet for a minute, feeling the restaurant moving around us. "How did you meet Maria?" I asked, taking another forkful of cake.

"At a—sort of dance club. It's in Queens." She smiled. "Maybe I'll take you sometime."

"Okay," I said, looking down at my empty cup.

Maria passed by and asked Ana if we wanted another.

"*Gracias*—I should probably—take her home," Ana said, looking at me inquiringly.

I shrugged, smiling helplessly.

"Or not?" She smiled back at me. "I'll have another if you want one," she said.

"You stay right there," said Maria with a big grin, taking our cups and leaving us in an embarrassed silence.

The strange thing was how happy I felt, just being quiet— even being embarrassed. It was a warm, secret kind of feeling, not at all the way I felt with Nate, like we were proving something. We were still smiling stupidly when we finally said good-bye to Maria. We didn't say a word to each other as we got into the van. I watched the streets, full of strangers, as she drove me home. It was late afternoon, and I knew classes would be over and Walter and Robert and Nate would all have dispersed from the institute for the evening. She pulled over across the street and we sat there again.

"So I'll see you soon?" she said finally.

"Yeah," I said, blushing, suddenly realizing what I was waiting for. I turned in a panic and opened the door.

"Hey," she said gently.

I turned back and she was just sitting there behind the wheel, looking at me with amusement, the way she had that first day, from the window of her cart. Before I knew it I leaned across to kiss her. Her mouth was so soft that I could feel my own mouth too, perfectly soft. I felt my whole body flush as I drew back.

"See you soon," I said, blind with embarrassment and excitement, my feet somehow landing on the pavement. I closed the door and ran straight across the street without looking back.

22

Walter was in the kitchen when I opened the door. I went giddily down the hall and found him gazing at a table loaded with plastic bags, and the doors of all the cabinets flung open. "I'm cooking dinner," he announced, taking a sip from a glass of wine.

I peered into one of the bags, relieved to have something to focus on. "What are you making?"

"Moroccan Fish Tagine," he said doubtfully. "From a recipe in the *Times* this morning."

"Do you need some help?" I asked, still trying to calm down. It was like trying to keep a pile of paper inside the dory on the trip across the bay. One minute it was in the boat and the next it was exploding into the air.

"Of course I do, dear. Did you think I was going to do this alone? I've been praying you would come through that door all evening."

"Do you have the recipe?" I asked, imagining myself circling back in the boat, the paper floating in the waves.

He lifted up various bags and patted his pockets in a little panic to find the recipe, already the worse for wear, folded several ways, and handed it to me. "I had to go to Brooklyn to get the ingredients," he said, watching as I looked it over.

"It doesn't look hard," I said, "as long as you're good at chopping."

"I'm terrific at chopping, as far as I can remember," he said.

He poured me a glass of wine and I set him up with a knife and a pile of vegetables at the kitchen table; I unwrapped the fish, which needed to be filleted, and felt myself zeroing in on the task.

"It's our anniversary tonight," he said, as he started in on the onions. "I doubt Robert will remember, but we usually go out, so I'm trying to surprise him."

"When's he supposed to get home?"

"I don't know, probably midnight, but I'm hoping that if he remembers, and he's planning on dinner, he'll be back at a reasonable hour."

I laughed. "How long have you been together?"

"As long as you've been alive, I think. Maybe longer. Arthur introduced us, at one of the parties he and your father threw—I know your father was there because at the end of the night when we were all too drunk to move he sang one of those Irish ballads of his, and totally stole the show." He sniffed, wiping his nose with his chopping hand. "So it was probably before you were born. Anyway, I was sure Robert had fallen for him already. In fact I'm sure everybody there *had* fallen for him," he said, putting the knife down to wipe the tears from his face. "He was a very beautiful man, your father. As evidenced by his daughter," he added, picking up his wineglass and taking a sip. "Not that he's not still beautiful—I'm sure he looks better than the two of us, rotting away here for twenty years."

I moved the knife under the clean white bones of the sole. I could feel the information he was giving me sucking at me like an undertow, my feet sinking further into the sand. *Irish ballads.* "Robert said you used to have parties," I said, trying to hold on.

"Arthur and your father did, yes, before Arthur got sick. I was still in graduate school. Robert was sort of a man about town in those days, or at least he thought he was—anyway, I'm sure he knew about those kinds of parties all over town. I thought I'd never seen anything so glamorous."

"I can't really imagine my father singing," I managed, pretending to concentrate on getting the relatively dull knife through the fish.

"He had to have a few drinks in him, of course," Walter said, wiping his nose. "But he has a beautiful voice. Didn't he sing to you when you were young? I bet he did and you can't remember it."

"I don't think so."

"It was the kind of singing," Walter continued, "which makes you think you heard it when you were a baby. Like a lullaby."

Just then my knife slipped; I didn't cut myself, but I felt a surge of frustration so strong that tears sprang to my eyes. "This knife is too dull," I said. "Didn't they ask you how you wanted them filleted at the store?"

"I thought they were fresher if you bought them like that," said Walter, startled at my tone.

I sniffed and turned to open a few drawers. "I bet there's a sharper knife somewhere," I said with my back to him, trying to calm down, but I was only crying more. I needed Mr. Blackwell, or someone anyway. When had everything gotten so confusing? I pulled at the drawers, looking in them, though I had cleaned them and reorganized them myself and knew there was no sharper knife. I ought to go over to Nate's, I told myself. I hadn't been there in two nights, and I hadn't told him when I'd be back.

"How many of these do you think I should cut?" said Walter, pushing his knife at a glistening pile of onions.

"Oh! That's more than enough," I said, laughing now, tears sliding down my face at last. Walter's eyes, too, were streaming with tears. "Onions!" I said, with another little laugh.

"Maybe you can have this knife," he said.

We traded knives and I felt myself begin to calm down. There was nothing so terrible about my father being able to sing. Mr. Blackwell used to sing, I suddenly remembered. Maybe that had made my father shy. "We had a friend who used to help us cook sometimes," I said. "He would have had these fish filleted in two minutes."

"I was wondering how your father could have been alone all those years," Walter said amiably, and I felt the fact of Mr. Blackwell floating up like smoke to the ceiling. "Should I peel the potatoes?" he asked.

"I'll do them," I said, turning back to my task. "This knife is much better."

"So has Nathaniel invited you to his sister's wedding yet?" he asked, settling into his wine.

"No," I said, looking back at him with surprise.

"Robert said he was going to. It'll be in some fabulous mansion in Connecticut, I hear. You'll have to give us all the details."

"Maybe he's not going to invite me," I said.

"I very much doubt that my dear. He's probably waiting for the right moment. Are you going over there tonight?"

"I don't know," I said. "I haven't seen him in a few days." I was watching my knife move under the potato skin as I began to peel: Mr. Blackwell always peeled them in one long strip. *Throw it over your shoulder,* he used to say, *and it'll land in the initials of the man you marry.*

"All the more reason then," Walter said, smiling. "He called twice for you today."

I helped him clear the table once we put the vegetables and the fish in a pot together to bake, and we got out a set of candles and candleholders to make it look fancier. Obviously he was counting on my leaving them to have dinner alone. I almost asked if he wouldn't mind my simply hiding in my room. But it was their anniversary after all, and they wanted the place to themselves.

"Do you want me to stay until he comes home?" I asked hopefully.

"No, no, dear. You go. Lord knows he might never show up."

I had a queer emptiness in me when I finally left and walked over to Nate's. The wine I'd drunk gave it a dizzy edge. I breathed in the cool night air, glad at least to be out of the house; the streets were becoming familiar. Ana's kiss seemed as if it had happened years before, in some other part of my life, and I walked faster, as if somehow I could keep ahead of it.

Nate took a few minutes before he buzzed me in, and when I

reached the top of the stairs I realized I'd woken him up. He stood at the door in his boxers, blinking at me. "Long time no see," he said.

"I helped Walter make dinner tonight for Robert," I said as if that would explain my absence.

He followed me inside, rubbing his hands over his face to wake himself up. "That's a first," he said.

"It's their anniversary."

"Is it?" He poured himself a glass of water from the tap, looking at me. "Did you have a little something to drink?"

"I guess so," I said. "What have you been doing?"

"We had to go on an emergency wedding cake tasting mission at two restaurants uptown." He opened the fridge and looked into it. "I saved a piece for you."

"Really?"

"Yeah," he said, smiling. Something about my sweet tooth amused him. "I don't have any wine to go with it," he said, taking out a big white box. "Oh—except champagne. I've had this in the fridge for like a year." He squinted at it. "It doesn't go bad, right?"

There was a single piece of cake inside the box, and it seemed as if I had never seen such a perfect slice—it was vanilla-white, and each layer was lined with sweet cream, and then raspberries, which seemed to be freshly crushed. Nate put it on a plate and handed it to me. "For you, madame," he said, "from Chef Antoine. Or something. Anyway, it's really good."

He popped the bottle unceremoniously and filled two wineglasses. "We decided the important thing was the frosting," he said. "They always overdo it at weddings, you know?"

I shook my head, my mouth full of cream. "I've never been to a wedding," I said, washing it down with the champagne.

He sat down across from me, holding his glass. "I was thinking you could come next weekend," he said. "Be my date."

I smiled, pretending surprise. There was nothing about him, really, that I didn't like. He was kind, and trustworthy, and handsome. Of all the girls I saw every day on the street, walking with their bags and their perfect hair and their easy laughs, he had chosen me. I leaned forward suddenly and kissed him, happy with champagne and sugar. He looked relieved.

"I don't really have anything to wear," I said, after we kissed some more, going back to the cake.

He laughed. "You can wear whatever you want. I think all your dresses are great. Anyway, my mother and my sister will be really glad I have a date."

I rolled my eyes, surprised at how much he was already cheering me up. "It's not like it would be hard for you to get a date," I said.

He grinned, used to this kind of flirting, and leaned back in his chair. "You don't think so?" he said. "I'm just a poor graduate student with a geeky thing for ancient Rome."

"You're handsome," I said honestly.

He looked pleased. "I'm going to have to hand her the ring," he said, as if he wanted even more attention, taking a bite of my cake.

"You'll be perfect," I said.

"Weddings are fun. Everybody dances."

"I don't think I even know how to dance."

"I bet you'll be good at it." He poured me a new glass of champagne.

I took a sip, thinking of my father singing.

"I bet you're the kind of person who's good at everything," he said, watching me.

I smiled as if everybody said that to me. I couldn't remember if there was anything I actually *was* good at. "I'm not good at telling the truth," I said with another smile, like a sphinx.

"Really?"

"No," I giggled. "I don't know. Doesn't everybody feel that way?"

"I don't think so," Nate said. "You *are* a little drunk, aren't you?"

"Maybe." I looked at the bubbles rising in my glass, and he got up from his seat to come and kiss me.

"Mmm," he said, kissing my neck. "I might just have to take advantage of you."

I giggled again, thinking it would be nice, not to talk.

23

I didn't go by Ana's cart the next day, or the day after. I stayed at Nate's until he left for Connecticut to help his mother and sister prepare. He bought me a train ticket to join him at the rehearsal dinner on Friday. I went back to the institute reluctantly, and did my best to avoid Robert and Walter for the next few days. I bought espressos at the café around the corner and I threw myself into the hypnotic undertaking in the library, counting cards by the hour.

Robert and Walter were uncharacteristically cheerful. One night I found them in the kitchen eating Chinese takeout, and Walter invited me in, waving his chopsticks over the open cartons—they had ordered too much. Robert, it turned out, had actually been to Nate's country house, where the wedding was taking place. He had been forced to play endless games of tennis and advised me that I would only be allowed on the court in whites.

"And what was it the mother said," Walter prompted him, "when you said you lived in the West Village?"

Robert pursed his lips mischievously and lifted his chin. "'In my day, there were nothing but hairdressers living there,'" he said. "'But I heard they all died of AIDS.'"

Walter cackled. "Can you imagine?"

"I never told Nathaniel about that, though," Robert added, plucking a dripping piece of broccoli from the carton. "He's not like that at all."

"Oh no," Walter said quickly. "Nate's always been very sweet." He filled a glass of wine for me and pushed it over. "Have you decided what you're going to wear?"

"My pink dress, I guess," I said, taking a sip.

"You're going to the rehearsal dinner too, right? So you'll need two."

"Don't let him frighten you," Robert said. "You should wear whatever you want."

"I'm not *frightening* her—I just want her to be prepared. Isn't Liz their precious only daughter? People like that spend zillions of dollars on weddings."

"Nate wouldn't have invited her if he wanted the most fashionable date in New York," Robert said. "Did he tell you you needed another dress?"

"No," I said, mildly insulted.

"We don't have to make her unrecognizable," Walter said, annoyed.

"My point, if you'd listen, is that we don't have to make her anything at all. She's perfectly charming the way she is, and Nate would be disappointed if she looked like a different person."

"How very insightful."

Robert leaned back in his chair. "Straight boys are not very complicated," he said, reaching for his wine.

The next morning I put on the pink dress and looked at it in the mirror. I had never, in fact, seen Julie wear it. It was true that it was not quite glamorous—it was cotton, and though it wasn't worn out, it didn't look new. But Nate had said he liked it plenty of times, and even Ana had said she liked it. I had gotten attached to it. Reluctantly, I took some money out of my envelope under the mattress and went to the café for an espresso, hoping to coax myself into shopping. I took my coffee to the window and opened a magazine, the way I had seen other women doing it, as if by instinct. Skinny girls in dresses filled the pages, languishing on couches, prancing down runways. The most formal event I had ever been to was a church dinner with Julie's family the week before Christmas. I had no idea what to wear to a wedding.

I found myself staring out at the street instead. Women went on busily, walking toward work, opening up the shops, hailing taxicabs. They probably all went to weddings, and certainly they all bought dresses—many of them were probably married themselves or, like Liz, about to get married. I thought of Maria, having her whole life, another already behind her; Ana, dragging her cart into the garage; my mother, slipping into the fog. And then there was me, sitting at the window, my life too tentative to even begin.

I closed the magazine and, as I got down from the stool, I realized where I was going. The feeling of leaning toward Ana in her van, like jumping out over the water off the town dock, came to me in a rush of courage.

The cart was a few blocks away, sparkling in the sun. A handful of customers were waiting loosely at the window. She saw me the minute I walked up, and as I waited I could feel the fact of our kiss filling the air around us.

"I thought you might not come back," she said, with a teasing smile, when all the customers were gone.

"I thought maybe you could tell me where to find a dress," I said, realizing how ridiculous I sounded the minute I said it.

"You gotta big date?"

"I have to go to a wedding."

"Sounds like a big date to me," she said, leaning her arms on the sill and looking at me with amusement. I looked down at the sidewalk, unable to meet her gaze, and she laughed. "At least you're not a good liar," she said, straightening up at the sight of a customer. "What kind of dress do you need to get?"

I shrugged and moved aside for the customer, who ordered a coffee and a buttered roll. She had it all in a paper bag in a minute. "Dresses aren't really my thing," she said when he was gone, leaning forward again in her perch. "But I do know someone who makes them." She glanced up the sidewalk and got out a cigarette. "When do you need it?"

"This weekend," I said.

She rolled her eyes. "You didn't leave it until the last minute or anything," she said as she lit her cigarette.

"I already have one dress," I protested. "I didn't know I'd need two."

She smiled, exhaling thoughtfully. "Coco can probably do it, unless he has some other job. I could pick you up when I'm done with work and take you up there."

"Today?"

"Yeah," she said, with a shrug.

That afternoon I was watching from the library window when she pulled up in front of the institute in her van. I hurried out to meet her, feeling her watching me as I came down the steps. She dangled a cigarette out the window; her hair was combed back and shined darkly as if she was fresh from the shower.

"Your house looks like a church," she said as I climbed into the passenger seat. "Did you say it was a library?"

"It's—more like a school," I said, buckling my seat belt. "But I work in the library."

She offered me a cigarette. She had changed into a fresh button-down shirt, short-sleeved, and a pair of black pants. I took the cigarette and she lit it for me.

"My dad sort of—founded it. I mean he used to work there." I wondered if I should have changed. At least brushed my hair. For some reason I felt myself wanting to tell her about Arthur, maybe because I was nervous, but also because I felt like I wanted to tell her everything. And now that I was in the van again, everything we did seemed only a matter of prelude to the next kiss.

We took the West Side Highway, and up past Fifty-second Street it rose up out of the city like a runway. The Hudson River stretched on one side, dark blue with the slight chill of the afternoon. On the other side of us it seemed buildings were pushing like weeds out of every inch of space. Cars poured off exits, in streams. The George Washington Bridge arced over the horizon. She turned up the music and we kept the windows down, smoking our cigarettes, flying up the highway.

The dressmaker's shop was on a busy street full of small shops in Ana's neighborhood, above a grocery store and advertised by the word TAILOR in pink neon lighting; WEDDINGS & COMMUNIONS was painted in neat letters in the next window.

Ana rang the bell and said something in Spanish before Coco buzzed us in. He came out onto the landing to look down at us with a humorless expression as we climbed the stairs. He was a fussy little man with a tiny mustache and the air of having been interrupted. Ana shook his hand respectfully and introduced me with equal seriousness; it occurred to me suddenly that she had dressed up not for me but for this encounter. He looked me up and down, frowning as she explained what we wanted, and then ushered us impatiently inside.

Ana flashed me a reassuring smile as we stepped into his apartment. He had turned the front room into a workshop: rolls of white fabric were tipped against the windows and pictures of women in dresses were tacked up in every available space. The sewing machine sat beside a long clean counter, the other end of which was a desk piled with notebooks and receipts. A curtained dressing room had been set up beside a rack of clothing awaiting alteration.

He began to ask Ana questions in Spanish and watched as she translated them: Was the wedding going to be inside or outside? During the daytime or evening?

I didn't know any of the answers and kept shrugging apologetically. "I think they were trying to get a tent for it," I volunteered, in case that would help.

Coco rolled his eyes. "*¿Estás segura que la invitaron?*"

"That's what she says," Ana answered in English. "I don't think *I'm* invited though."

"We all have our own parties to go to, dear," he said, primly, in perfect English, putting on a pair of reading glasses and picking a worn notebook from the desk. He opened it on top of the counter. It was full of dresses he'd made: some had started with sketches he'd drawn himself and some came from magazine pages; the majority were made from professional patterns. Stapled to the sketch or glossy photograph were pictures of his customers—plump older ladies and smiling little girls, big wedding pictures with whole rows of bridesmaids, Polaroids of women standing in his shop, the light of the camera's flash glancing off the mirror. At the bottom of each page was a number that matched the manila envelope containing the pattern he had cut: the envelopes were arranged neatly on shelving above the counter.

He relaxed a little more when he saw how impressed I was, and went through the notebook with care, describing the front and back of a dress where there was no picture, relating the failures of certain materials, the risks of certain colors. It was Ana who finally chose the one we went with—it was backless, with two strips of material that came over the chest and tied behind the neck, a long waist and a loose skirt. The model who was wearing it was tall and brown-skinned, her hair smoothed over her scalp and sculpted into elaborate waves on top of her head. Her dress was black but Ana thought mine should be green, to match my eyes.

Coco brought out various patches of material and held them up to my face so they could compare, and then finally he brought out a splash of thick red silk left over from another customer and laid it across my shoulder.

He stood back and smiled. Ana whistled.

"Won't it be hard to sew?" I said nervously, stroking it absently as I turned to look at myself in the mirror. It felt like water.

"*¿Es carisimo?*" asked Ana, leaning back against the desk.

He shrugged. "I can give it to you for a good price."

"You like it?" She looked at me.

"I guess so," I said, confused. "Isn't it—too bright though?" Coco had already begun quietly measuring around my shoulders, waist, and chest, his mind made up.

"You'll look great in it," Ana answered, straightening up.

She blared her music as we drove back downtown, and though she turned often to smile at me, I wondered if she felt she had gone too far. It already felt familiar to be sitting beside her; we were hurtling hopelessly toward something we both were trying to recognize. It was just getting dark when we got back to the institute, and she stopped the car and waited for me to get out.

"Thanks for taking me up there," I said, suddenly embarrassed.

"Sure," she said, smiling again.

24

It took me all morning to buy a pair of high heels on Eighth Street, which was lined with shoe stores. In the end I settled for black, with a thin strap across the ankle and a small buckle. When Ana picked me up in the afternoon I tottered out to the van wearing them with one of the miniskirts Nate had bought me.

"Maybe Coco can teach you how to walk in those," she said when I got in beside her.

Coco could hardly contain his excitement when we arrived. I towered over him in my new shoes. He made Ana stay in the workshop and took me down the hall to the bathroom, where he told me to put the dress on and come out when I was ready for him to tie it up around the neck. I took off my T-shirt and skirt and only after I'd gotten the dress over my head did I realize I needed to take off my bra too. I tied the straps clumsily over my breasts and stepped out into the hall. He considered me for barely a minute before he made me turn around so he could retie the straps. Then he took a tuck at the waist and turned me around to frown at me again. He stood back.

"Let's see you take a few steps," he said. I walked forward, and the skirt swayed gently around my legs, flashing with light. He looked down at my shoes. "You'll have to learn to walk in those. Did you buy them today? Put your shoulders back and pick up your chin. That's right, look ahead—just remember you're walking on your toes. Relax your calf muscles."

I felt suddenly like a dancer. I was tall and my arms felt free and strong. The skirt played gently over my thighs. He sighed, turning me around to take in the waist again while I balanced myself against the wall.

"I find the perfect woman with the perfect body to wear this dress," he muttered through the pins in his mouth, "and she can't even walk."

Ana stood up when I walked in and made room for me to walk over to the mirror. I glanced at myself shyly and then looked back at her.

"What do you think?" she said.

I shrugged, not sure what to do with my hands. "It feels pretty nice," I said.

"It looks pretty nice," she said.

Coco sewed the rest of the adjustments while we waited, and put the dress in a garment bag for Ana to carry. When I attempted to pay he looked surprised. "She already took care of it," he said, as if it were obvious.

Ana gestured for me to go ahead of her out the door and I thanked him and followed her.

"I didn't mean for you to pay," I said as soon as we got onto the sidewalk.

"Don't worry about it," she said.

"How about if I take you out to dinner then?" I said when we got into the van.

She offered me a cigarette and took one for herself. "Your neighborhood or mine?"

"Yours," I said playfully, looking down the street.

She shook her head, her mouth pursed, lighting her cigarette. "If it's my neighborhood I'm paying," she said, exhaling.

"Then mine."

"Then we have to go back to my house for a second so I can change."

"Really?" I said.

"Yeah," she said, pulling out of the parking space. "I gotta look *respectable.*"

Her building was squeezed between rows of brownstones on a narrow street a few minutes away from the dressmaker's shop, but we had to drive around the block for a while to find a parking spot. It was late in the afternoon and people were walking home holding plastic bags of groceries, wheeling carts full of meticulously folded laundry. On one corner by a grocery store a few boys bounced a ball into the street in front of us.

Nearby, a group of boys sat on a stoop watching us circling. Two of them were wearing thick gold chains around their necks like medals—they lounged comfortably, like they knew they could be noticeable if they felt like it: in front of them was an empty parking spot, allowing them full view of the street. Ana passed over the spot the first time, but the second time she turned down her music and pulled in. They watched her deft parking without seeming to look at us at all, but at the sound of my heels on the pavement we came into sharp focus. Ana slammed her door and got out on the sidewalk in front of them. One of the boys with a necklace said something to her in Spanish, which she pretended not to hear.

I hurried to catch up, trying to stay steady. "White girl looks like she needs a taste of something real," one boy said to another, in a conversational tone.

"Hey, Mami," said the boy who had spoken in Spanish, "you forgot your dick?" They all laughed.

Ana flushed and kept walking. I strode along beside her, terrified. "Fucking assholes," she said, under her breath, without slowing down.

I wanted to erase it, and tell her that she shouldn't care—that I didn't care—but it felt so terrible that I knew I did care, and so did she. When we got to her building she opened the outer door with her keys and we walked up the stairs in punished silence. I couldn't tell if she was angry or if she was going to cry. I wanted to be angry but instead I had a strange, hollow feeling inside me—a kind of disbelief—and I kept turning the moment over in my mind, as if I could correct it somehow, or as if I'd misremembered it.

When she let me into the apartment we moved around each other with embarrassment. "I'll be real quick," she said, ducking into what I assumed was her bedroom.

The living room was small with a large flowered couch and a matching armchair taking up most of the space. It was lavishly decorated but scrupulously neat, a few stray toys the only evidence of her sister's children; a small kitchen extended behind it, with a picture of the Virgin Mary on the patterned wall, struck by afternoon light. Ana must have known no one would be home; it was hard to imagine the whole family inside such a small space. I got up to look at the miniature skyline of picture frames above the television. I found a photo of Ana's communion in a big gold frame: she was looking miserably at the camera, dwarfed by her oversize dress, her hair hopelessly frizzy.

"That's the only picture they have of me in a dress," she said, coming out of her room in a fresh T-shirt and pants and sitting down on the couch to put on her shoes. "So of course it's the one they keep out."

I turned away, not sure if she wanted me to look at it, and sat down beside her with my hands in my lap. She took a deep breath and leaned back like she was suddenly exhausted.

"Maybe we should have a beer," she said.

I reached for her hand and she looked up at me apologetically. "At least I didn't get the shit beaten out of me," she said.

I raised her hand to my lips and kissed it. She looked at me intently and I leaned forward and kissed her on the lips. We were kissing very gently at first: then we'd draw away, and look at each other, like we were both swimming in the same feeling—of needing each other—and then we'd start over again. It turned into a sort of rhythm, and then grew urgent, and slipped back again, into a soft pattern. I put my hand up to touch her face and as she turned toward me I reached down to her breasts.

Somehow then we were lying on the couch: I was lying on top of her. She was warm and clean and her body was firm under mine. I put my hand under her shirt and felt the smooth skin of her stomach, and suddenly I wanted nothing more than to be inside her. I left her kisses and leaned down to kiss along the top of her pants. When I looked up at her again she was watching me with a wistful kind of tenderness, and as I pulled her pants over her hips she lifted herself on the couch to let me take them down. She was wearing white cotton underwear, and I kissed the pungent place between her legs, feeling the springy hair underneath, before I pulled them down too, to reveal a broad black triangle of pubic hair.

I looked up at her, afraid to touch it. She took my hand and put it between her legs, pressing it inside to feel the place where she was slippery and full. Something broke, something broke in me. I had never felt anything so soft. I touched it and stroked it until I was leaning over her, stroking her faster and faster, pushing my fingers deeper, moving in and out of her, thrusting, until she cried out and curled up, her whole body snapping like elastic, and I felt a wave of heat emptying me like a sob.

I don't know how long we lay there in the dark, or when she began to stroke my hair away from my temples. I felt as if I'd been asleep for hours. But I know I was sitting up, dizzily taking a sip of my beer and handing hers to her when we heard voices in the hall. She jerked up her pants in less time than it took me to realize what was happening, and as I stood, loose-limbed and strange, she pointed with a mad kind of urgency toward the bathroom door.

I had only just made it across the room and through the door when the voices came in from hallway and rattled the living room. I didn't move from my place behind the door, holding myself perfectly still. I heard another woman's voice joining the others, the light cadence of a child among them. After a few minutes I looked around me. Everything was pink: the sink, the tub, the toilet, the bar of soap on the sink, the shower curtain tucked neatly into the tub. I felt oddly calm. I heard the television turned on, the female voices shouting over it, then that music Ana played in her van carrying through the wall.

Just as I was wondering whether to lock the door, it opened. A small child, concentrating on his own adventure, crawled toward the edge of the pink tub. When he looked up he was surprised to see me—but no more surprised, I suppose, than he had been to find that the door pushed open, or that the pink bathroom mat was soft. He sat back on his diapered bottom and gave me a serious look. I smiled at him and he watched me a little uncertainly, but when I smiled again he smiled back, willing to be charmed. My new courage hadn't gone away; this seemed to me a strange sign that I belonged. I made a face, and he laughed, and no sooner had he made the noise than I heard Ana's voice outside the door.

I was just in time to block the door from smacking into him. "Go now!" she said, her face lit with panic. "I'll meet you outside."

It seems possible that I had never picked up a child in my life before that moment, but I scooped him up and deposited him into her arms before I walked out of the bathroom. A young woman came out of the kitchen at the same moment and before she could say a word Ana had transferred the child into her arms and put her finger over her lips.

"*¿Quién es ella?*" I heard the girl say, as I let myself out the door. I stood for a few minutes on the street outside the building but I wasn't sure whether or not I should be seen. The boys on the corner were gone. I crossed to the other side of the street and walked back to where I could watch the door. When Ana came out she looked around coolly and then headed in my direction, her face casual, her hands thrust into her pockets. I took in her dark messy hair, her loose cotton shirt, the jeans I had unzipped earlier. She walked up to the other side of the car I was lurking behind.

"Wanna go to dinner?" she said across the hood, smiling.

Neither of us knew where to go to dinner downtown. I didn't want to take her to any of the places I'd been to with Nate, and I didn't know how to get to them by car anyway. We parked in the West Village and walked around, trying to get a sense of what the other wanted, and then we walked into a place with a garden in back and the murmur of people. I ordered a bottle of wine. We had salads, and a meal, and ordered another bottle of wine, even though we were already drunk.

She told me about the first time she kissed a girl and the first time she kissed a boy; she told me about when she learned to speak English and when she started cutting her hair short and the first time her sister got pregnant; she told me about her mother's family in Santo Domingo and her father's mistresses on the north coast.

I told her how I used to want to be a tree and she laughed. "Why didn't you want to be a person?" she asked.

I shrugged. "I was already a person."

"You didn't like it?"

"I don't know," I said. I looked at her. "I didn't always like it so much I guess. Haven't you ever wanted to be something else?"

"Sure," she said. "Like a rich person. All trees do is stand there."

"They see everything."

"Yeah, but they can't do anything about it."

"I know, but they don't want to," I said. "I mean they're not sad, and they don't need to remember anything. They're just growing."

She took a sip of her wine. "Were you sad when you were a kid?"

"Not really," I said. "My father was, though. I mean when I was growing up." The waitress came to clear our plates. "I found out he used to sing, at parties."

She smiled. "You sure he wasn't drunk?"

"No, he's drunk plenty at home and he never sings." It came out more harshly than I had meant it. "Supposedly he has a really beautiful voice."

"Maybe he should have been a rock star," she said, refusing my seriousness.

I smiled despite myself, feeling the melancholy pull of the wine. "Do you want dessert?" I asked her. What I wanted was to tell her everything: how sometimes he hardly spoke to me for days, and sometimes that didn't even matter because I knew what he needed anyway. Once when he was asleep on the couch I kissed him on the forehead and he didn't wake up. And then when I kissed him on the lips he just frowned and rubbed his nose, as if he'd felt a fly. And once, in the middle of the night, I'd heard him crying—an awful, thin sound. I'd stayed awake until it stopped, feeling as if I was crying myself.

Ana was watching me. "What do you want to be now?" she said gently.

"I don't know," I said, smiling at her. "An artist, maybe."

"Really?"

"Yeah," I said, shy. "What do you want to be?"

"A rich person," she said again. "Or anyway someone who doesn't have to live with my family."

"How about you stay with me tonight then?" I said, snatching the bill before she could get it.

25

It seemed we were barely asleep before she was out of bed and dressed again, giving me a kiss goodbye. When I woke up a few hours later the red dress was slung over my desk chair like a piece of a dream. It was noon and I'd told Nate I'd get to Connecticut by three. I got up and showered and put on my jeans and packed my two dresses into a knapsack. Ana had left a note for me on a page torn out of my sketchbook, written in charcoal pencil. "Have fun in the dress," it said. Below that she had written her address and phone number. *Ana Mones.* I put her note in my bag too and then went downstairs and cooked myself some eggs. Robert showed me how to get to Grand Central Station, and an hour later I was walking across the marble lobby and down onto the platforms for the trains to Connecticut.

Nate was waiting for me on the platform at Mystic, wearing a bright red sweater, his shoulders hunched against the seaside chill. I had slept the whole trip and I watched blearily as he strode forward to the gate. He kissed me on the cheek and took my knapsack from me as we walked to the car. We drove through the fussy town in minutes and soon there were salt marshes stretched out on either side of us, spotted with black ducks.

"Where's the ocean?" I asked him.

He smiled. "You'll see it when we get to the house," he said. "I can't wait for you to meet everybody."

"I should maybe—get a cup of coffee," I said, without really meaning to, and he laughed.

"They're not that bad. I'll make you one there."

I smiled, and he took my hand. We went across a small bridge, which turned out to be part of their driveway. White oaks sheltered the sandy circle at the end of it, landscaped with huge rhododendrons. Motorboats were dry-docked discreetly beside a smaller house that Nate referred to as "the cottage."

We went in through the kitchen door. Liz and another blond woman I took to be Mrs. Stoddard were filling out place cards with their backs to a wall of picture windows, outside of which a big white tent was being put up. In spite of the autumn chill, both women were wearing tennis clothes. Liz gave me a little wave, but stayed where she was sitting, and Mrs. Stoddard came around the table to shake my hand. Her socks, I noticed distractedly, came just to the brim of her shoes and had little yellow balls attached to them. I felt my blue jeans being examined for the worse: the girlish absurdity of her outfit only seemed to enhance her authority. She had Nate's regal features and Liz's shining blond hair, a magazine smile. "How was your trip?" she asked.

"Has anyone seen my sledgehammer?" Nate's father interrupted, coming into the kitchen. "I think we should give those tent pegs a couple more knocks into the ground."

"Come meet Miranda, Hal," said his wife.

He came over to shake my hand. "Nice to meet you," I said, feeling them all watching me.

"Got a good grip," he said to his audience. He winked at me, not the way Mr. Blackwell used to, but the way people do in high school musicals, when they're singing a song with a joke in it. "Nate tells me your father's some kind of genius, isn't that right?"

"I'm afraid the tent's going to fall down anyway, Daddy," Liz said, looking out the window. "They told me they're having a hurricane in Florida."

"It's a hurricane *warning,* Princess."

"I'm sure the people who put up the tent know what they're doing," said Mrs. Stoddard, sitting back down with Liz. "Anyway, I thought you were going to move the boats out of the driveway first."

"I thought the boatyard was sending someone," Mr. Stoddard said, putting the sledgehammer over his shoulder.

"You're not a vegetarian are you, Miranda?" she asked me, ignoring him. "Lizzie thought you might be."

"No," I said, feeling as if I should have been.

"Tink," Mr. Stoddard said, "do you mean I'm going to have to call Parker myself?"

"I don't know what has to happen for you to move those boats," she said, going back to her place cards. "I told you to leave them in the water until the wedding was over. We could call the boatyard, but that's up to you, and your mother will be arriving in an hour."

"Nate," Liz said in what I thought for a second was a parody of her mother's voice, "would you mind calling over to where the

Vances are staying to make sure the other groomsmen know about the rehearsal?"

"I think we should send him over to the club, Lizzie," Mrs. Stoddard intervened as her husband stalked off. "Marjorie has some idea about the club not having enough ice for the dinner."

"She doesn't have some idea, Mom, their ice machine is broken. And it won't take that long for him to call over there."

"Why don't you do it yourself then," Nate said without an ounce of exasperation, bringing a carton of orange juice out of the refrigerator and pouring himself a glass without offering any to me. He drank it down thirstily, as if he was suddenly remembering how long he had been craving it. For a minute, I saw him as I imagined his mother must have, as an overgrown boy. "How many bags of ice does she need?" he said, looking over at her.

"You can take some money from my purse." She nodded at the leather bag on the counter.

"Do you want to come with me?"

I looked up in surprise, having almost forgotten that I was standing in the middle of them. "Sure," I said brightly, as if I would have been equally happy to have been left behind. Nate rummaged in his mother's bag the same way he opened the refrigerator, stuffing a few bills into his pocket and gesturing for me to follow him back out the door.

"Don't forget that we have to be here to rehearse at six," Liz yelled as the screen door slammed behind us.

I ran to catch up with him. "Who are the Vances?" I asked.

"Geoffrey's parents," he said, annoyed.

I wished I'd remembered to ask him again for the coffee. "Is it always like this?" I said before I knew it.

"Like what?"

"Busy?" I suggested.

"Well, the wedding is tomorrow," he said, climbing into the driver's seat, the muscles on either side of his jaw standing out oddly.

I'd said the wrong thing, of course. I looked out the window as we started back out across the marsh. Ana seemed like a dream, or some kind of crazy misadventure. Nate was quiet, concentrating on driving. He had always been kind, and this was his family, after all, whether he liked it or not. He loved them, the way I loved my father, and he was doing his best for them.

"You okay?" he said, reaching out for my hand.

"Yeah," I said, giving his hand a squeeze, like a promise. "You might just have to tell me what to do occasionally. I'm— I'm not really used to families."

"You'll be fine," he said, patting my thigh before he took his hand back for driving. "I'm really glad you came. It's just a little crazy right now."

We went past the railroad station and through the town, headed toward a marina. It made me nervous to be around people who were busy, I told myself. They always seemed to be women. My father was never busy. When he was working he was concentrating. If anybody was busy it was Mr. Blackwell, but everything he did had a kind of manly focus, whether he was filling a gas tank, deboning a fish, braiding my hair, or washing blood from the deck. I could picture him, careful and absorbed. Ana was like that too, I thought, looking out the window. When I kissed her I felt like I was inside that place, that place she was concentrating from—as if we were both there, alone in the quiet.

"What are you thinking about?" Nate's voice asked.

"Nothing," I said, turning to give him a smile.

He slowed and pulled the car into the parking lot of the Yacht Club, where he said he used to teach sailing. It was a large, gray-shingled building with a porch overlooking a long white pier stretching out into a harbor dotted by empty moorings. An American flag snapped vigorously at the end of the pier.

Nate ran inside to ask Geoffrey's mother how much ice she needed. I stayed in the car looking at the sailboats stacked on the side of the parking lot, identical white hulls locked into tidy racks. He'd told me about summers here, making out in the sail loft and driving boats around on the water all day with girls asking him to put lotion on their backs. He'd told me about all his girlfriends: the one at boarding school who dyed her hair black and the one from California whom he'd met in France when he did a bike trip there one summer. And the one his mother liked so much—Sarah, who was in law school. The information came back to me in vague sequences. Nothing in my own life had seemed interesting enough to tell him—but then nothing I'd told Ana had seemed interesting either, until she was the one listening.

Nate tapped on my window and motioned for me to roll it down. I fiddled uselessly with the little switches on the door. Finally it lowered slowly down between us. He looked impatient. "She doesn't know anything about the ice machine," he said, "but she has some problem with the flowers." I looked at him blankly. "Maybe you could help her? I think I should get ice."

He pointed me up the sandy wooden steps to a room as big and empty as the harbor, hollowed out, it seemed, by endless summers of shouting children. The walls were decorated with flags and faded charts, white billboards spotted with tacks. Caterers in black pants and white tops were silently rolling huge round tables into the center of the room. I watched as they shook out the tablecloths, smoothing them over with a broad sweep of one hand. A woman I assumed was Mrs. Vance stood at the back of the room, already dressed for dinner in a knit suit with a belt. Her hair was styled into a luxuriant, chestnut-colored helmet on the top of her head. She was standing next to a table crowded with flower baskets, as if she was guarding them.

"Are you Miranda?" she whispered as I approached her. "I don't know why I didn't ask someone to come over with me, but you know we have too much to do anyway. Mrs. Stoddard was going to help me, but she has so much on her mind, I didn't want to bother her."

"Nate said you thought there was something wrong with the flowers?" I said. The bouquets were arranged with greens and baby's breath in baskets along with bright roses and lovely orange lilies, each bloom auspiciously open.

"Oh! Yes." She took a sip of a drink that was sitting beside her. "Mrs. Stoddard had them sent here this morning. They're *centerpieces,*" she added, looking at them with suspicion.

"What's wrong with them?"

"Geoffrey thinks roses are sentimental," she whispered. "I told her that months ago."

There were certainly a lot of roses in them, if you looked at it that way. "Maybe we should take them out," I suggested.

Her eyes lit up. "Do you think Mrs. Stoddard would mind? I don't want to step on anyone's toes. It was their idea to have the dinner here. I would much rather have had it in the city. These rehearsal dinners"—she lowered her voice again—"are supposed to be put on by the groom's family, but it's not as if we've any say. Mr. Stoddard wanted to have the whole wedding at the golf club."

"I doubt Mrs. Stoddard would notice the roses," I said, trying to look thoughtful.

She gave me a mischievous smile, and we went to work plucking them out. The florist, we discovered, had cleaned off all the thorns, and it didn't take long to strip all thirty bouquets. We put the unwanted roses in a trash barrel by a bar that the caterers were unpacking, and Mrs. Vance borrowed a few cocktail napkins to cover them up so that Mrs. Stoddard wouldn't see them.

"She's very particular," she whispered, turning back to the bar. "Would you like something? There's not much ice."

After we had distributed the baskets on the tables we noticed there were a few bald spots in the flower arrangements where you could see the spongy green base, and I made another round, rearranging the greens, while Mrs. Vance got me a vodka tonic to match her own. By the time Nate came back with the seating chart and place cards, I was feeling very fond of her, and stayed by her side as she went about inspecting the room.

"Do you think," she muttered, "that we can put Dr. Stevens next to this Leila Strom? He's a plastic surgeon."

"I don't know Ms. Strom," I said, as if I knew everybody else.

"Well, supposedly she's a feminist," she whispered. "I don't really know her either but I think she plays tennis with Mrs. Stoddard; she's one of their law firm friends."

"Who's Robert Neill Pursley?" I asked, looking at the next name.

"Oh, he's an old family friend," she said. "He'll get along with anyone. My husband calls him 'the confirmed bachelor.' I could put him next to Minnie Baxter, I guess. She'll think he's flirting with her."

Nate coughed behind her at this point, and muttered about our having to change for the dinner. Mrs. Vance was so intent on the cards she hardly noticed us leaving. Another focused person, I thought, making a tipsy parallel. When we got back to the house the wedding party was in the kitchen mixing cocktails for each other. I changed into my pink dress and had another vodka tonic while the priest pushed them around out in the backyard, showing them how to line up for the ceremony. The wind had picked up even more fiercely, and the backs of the groomsmen's blazers were flipping up like little ducktails. The bridesmaids crossed their arms and huddled together in their tiny cardigans, their cheeks pinked by the salt air.

It turned out I was seated between Nate's godparents, George and Angela Night, which Mrs. Vance had assured me was "a very good sign." They beamed at me readily enough as we picked up our elaborately folded napkins to smooth them on our laps, but their smiles faltered as I explained that I was "more like a secretary" than a fellow, as Nate was, at the institute.

"Where did you go to college?" asked Mr. Night, trying to disguise his concern.

"I haven't," I said. The cocktails had made me cheerful but the wine was making me feel exhausted and unvarnished.

"Your father's been working on a translation, isn't that right?" said Mrs. Night, trying to rescue me. "Nate made him sound like a very interesting man."

I shrugged. "He likes to be alone," I said.

Mr. Night nodded sympathetically; Mrs. Night looked at her salad as if she had discovered bugs in the lettuce. I wondered how I had found so much to talk about with Mrs. Vance. Mrs. Night complimented me on my dress again, and suddenly it occurred to me that she didn't like it at all. I thought of the red dress I'd hung up in the small room Nate had given me for myself ("Don't worry, they know you'll sneak up to my room anyway") and knew she wouldn't like that one either.

When the dessert came each of the groomsmen began standing up to say a few words about Geoffrey's unfinished novel. Nate stood up and blushed very sweetly before he spoke. "I probably have more experience getting bossed around by Liz than anyone else in this room," he began, and everyone roared with delight. Mr. Night, who had maintained a monopoly on the red wine while the rest of the table circulated the white, leaned over to whisper, "He's a real firecracker!" hotly in my ear.

"But those of you who saw us growing up," Nate continued, "also know how many times Liz managed, on and off the race course, to keep me out of trouble. I'll never forget being in first place at the Junior Regatta and rounding the windward buoy wrong; Liz argued with me about it for the whole downwind leg and when we figured out I was disqualified she didn't even say I told you so—she took off her life jacket and dove into the water to let me sail home myself, since that was what I wanted to do anyway." Nate looked rather stricken as he told this anecdote, but the crowd exploded again with laughter, as if Liz's cruelty had long been taken for granted.

"When Liz first met Geoffrey," Nate started in again, "she

told me he was the one, and I believed her. . . ." He was handsome, standing there speaking in his strong voice, but his doting toast began to remind me of the first time we'd had lunch, and Liz had gotten all his attention. When he raised his glass to his sister and his new brother-in-law, people had tears in their eyes; I clinked my own glass with the Nights', trying to avoid the smug looks they were offering me. I wished I was proud instead. Something inside me had shrunk.

Families, it seemed to me, as Nate's parents got up and insisted he join them in a little song, liked to humiliate each other. Julie's family always used to laugh at her brother's painful tantrums; there was something sinister about how everybody was forced to participate. Even Nate now was smiling and clapping his hands, belting out the refrain:

Tomorrow is the wedding day, do dah do day
Our little Lizzie is to be given away, do dah do day
We wish we could make her stay, do dah do day
For she's our darling girl. . . .

I watched all the guests join in for the last chorus. It seemed to me that they all believed that if you followed their rules cheerfully, and you sailed and played tennis and drank your cocktails, you would get everything you wanted: a big bright mansion on the bluffs of the Connecticut shore, a beautiful daughter, and a big white tent in the backyard.

Nate was flushed with good spirits when we finally got into the car to drive home, and he kissed me for a while before he put the keys in the ignition, running his hands over the front of my pink dress.

"My godparents liked talking to you," he said as he turned on the headlights. Two bridesmaids, squatting to pee at the edge of the parking lot, were caught in the light and looked up like frightened rabbits, but he was busy with the gearshift. "Angela says you're a real keeper."

One of the girls scurried behind a car, hysterical with laughter, while the other fell over in the dark. "What does that mean?" I said, tired of all the antics.

"You know," he said, looking over his shoulder as he backed the car up, "like a fish."

26

The pressure in the air increased during the night, and by morning the sky was black and angry. I put on my jeans and went down to the kitchen to hide next to the coffee pot while the family bustled about. Nate and his father went for a run and came back looking as if they'd been swimming in their jogging clothes. They stood by the sink together, guzzling glasses of water, their white T-shirts transparent with sweat, chest hair plastered underneath in patterns. We all agreed that it was about to rain.

"I'll take Miranda into town to get some umbrellas," Nate said, refilling his water glass.

Mr. Stoddard nodded. "We'll be needing them," he said, with a wink at me.

The tent was shaking as we left the house, the trees around the driveway beginning to rush with wind. As we got into the car I felt the hint of electricity that comes before a storm.

"It will be nice," Nate said, wiping his sweaty forehead on a fresh shirt, "when the rain clears this air out."

The sky rolled dolefully across the marshes as we drove into town. Birds grouped in the grass. Nate was thoughtful after his exercise. "I never thought my dad would really get into the wedding stuff," he said, "but he's really pulling out all the stops." He looked at me. "It's a big thing for him, I think. I get the feeling he's having kind of a hard time giving her away. It's probably like you and your father. I always get the feeling you're really close."

I shifted in my seat. "Sort of. He's not really so good at telling me what he's thinking, though."

"Right," Nate said, nodding. "It's such classic masculine stuff. You'd think they'd be embarrassed to be such a cliché."

I looked back at the marsh. *My father is not a cliché,* I thought irritably. He would never wink, or call me "princess," or allow hundreds of people to laugh at my foibles over dinner. Nate flicked on the wipers, though the rain was only just beginning to speckle the windshield. I looked over at him and he smiled and leaned back comfortably in his seat. I thought of Ana guiding her van into the traffic, her shoulders hunkered down as if the van was part of her compact body, reaching for the music, drumming the steering wheel. *Bachata.*

"I was thinking," Nate said, as the windshield wipers squinched back and forth, "maybe you could buy some stockings."

"Stockings?" I looked at him.

"Whatever you call them—nylons, for your legs. While I get the umbrellas." He looked over at me. "It'll probably be cold," he added, when I continued to look perplexed.

I hated stockings, the way they pushed all the hairs on my legs in the wrong direction, and the way they drooped at the crotch. I hated the tight feeling of them on my hips and stomach and the way they made my feet sweat. I stared ahead, watching the storm clouds lower, thick as featherbeds. "I don't think I'll mind the cold," I said.

He gave a shrug. "We'll just see if they have them," he said, turning the car into the parking lot.

In fact they had a whole rack of them beside the register, in little cases shaped like eggs. "Which kind should I get?" I asked him unhappily, looking at the rows of colors: Misty Silk, Utter Reliance, Sassy Support, Soft Black, Nude, Ivory, Suntan. He looked over my shoulder at the picture of a woman with long legs lying seductively on top of the rack. "What color is your dress?"

"Red," I said.

His eyebrows shot up. "Really?" he said, smiling, as if I'd brought it as a favor for him. Which in fact I had.

"Yeah," I said, suddenly realizing I didn't want to wear it at all.

"Why don't you get Nude? They probably go with everything. What size are you?"

By the time we got back to the family compound, it had begun to pour. Liz was in the cottage with the bridesmaids and the hairdresser, and Nate's mother was still in her tennis skirt, panicking. They were supposed to have been ready for photographs half an hour before, and she needed to find a basket for the umbrellas. Nate found one for her and told her I'd strip all the plastic cases while they went upstairs to shower. He gave me a kiss and hurried upstairs. I slid each of the cases off one by one, feeling the anticipation all around me in the empty house.

Afterward I went down to my bedroom and showered, combed my hair, and put on the stockings and the dress. I looked at myself in the mirror and tried to adjust the straps, but my breasts seemed huge and the dress seemed tiny. Without the clutter of Coco's shop, the excitement of Ana looking at me, it looked like a costume left over from a carnival, a dress for a dancer under a thousand lights.

I went up to Nate's bedroom and knocked with a sinking feeling in my stomach. He opened the door naked, rubbing a towel vigorously over his wet hair.

"Whoa," he said as I stepped inside, letting the towel go limp. "That is one sexy dress."

"Do you like it?" I said nervously.

"Well, Jesus, it's—I mean, you look gorgeous. Where did you get it?"

"At a dressmaker's," I said, with a new wave of despair. "I got it made."

"You got it made?" His own outfit was laid out on the bed, pressed and ready to go. He pulled on his underwear and then shook out the pants, sliding them on expertly and buttoning them at the waist. I watched as he buttoned up his crisp shirt, tucking everything in, cinching the belt tight. I felt already like I missed him, this handsome man. I had already gone off to the carnival.

"You might be cold, though," he said, taking a pair of cuff links off his bureau and frowning as he put them on. "My mom probably has a shawl or something."

"Okay," I said faintly.

"We were supposed to be taking the pictures ten minutes ago, but I bet she's still in her bedroom. I have to get her to tie my tie anyway," he said, flipping up his collar and putting the bright red bow tie around his neck to get it ready. "Why don't you come with me so she can see the dress?"

The parents' bedroom was just down the hall from Nate's. Mrs. Stoddard was sitting in her bra and underwear, blow-drying her hair. Nate escorted me gently toward her and started shouting at her about a shawl. She had her hair combed over her face and when she finally flipped it over she looked at us in the mirror. She combed her hair into place and turned off the hair dryer immediately.

"Well, hello, pretty lady!" Nate's father exclaimed, coming in from their adjoining bathroom, his bow tie in place. "She matches our bow ties!"

"I was thinking maybe she might be a little cold," Nate repeated to his mother. "Do you think you have a shawl or something she could wear?"

His mother sighed and looked at me impatiently. "We were supposed to be photographed fifteen minutes ago," she said, turning back to her mirror to adjust her bangs. She opened a bottle of mascara. "She can wear whatever she likes but I can't choose it for her," she said, pressing back her eyelashes with the strange little brush and blinking uncontrollably. When she was done with her makeup she put on her dress, a wispy, shapeless, flowery blue affair, which swung down around her shins. She picked up her hair and turned around so Nate could zip her up.

"Don't look so frightened, dear," she said when she found herself facing me. "We'll get you covered up. You're welcome to anything in that bureau drawer over there."

Then she turned to her husband, who was still standing by the bathroom door: "I told the photographer we'd set up in the library."

"Why don't we do it in the boat room?" Nate said, watching

...ok into the mirror again to make sure the dress
...ged her makeup.

...wanted it in the library," said Mr. Stoddard.

..."n't want to get into it with her," Mrs. Stoddard added,
...hair. "We could have done this whole thing at the

...yway, we should go down. You'll just have to see

...find," she said to me with a teachery kind of smile

...ck up. "Okay?"

...ed over to kiss me and I felt his parents watching

...a frank mixture of tolerance and anxiety. "We'll see you

...in the tent, Miranda," said Mr. Stoddard.

I stood there in the empty room after they left. The air had
been sweetened with Mrs. Stoddard's makeup, Mr. Stoddard's
soapy shower, the burning smell of the hair dryer. All the closets
were flung open, Mrs. Stoddard's dresses and Mr. Stoddard's
shirts in neat colored rows. I could hear the wedding party col-
lecting downstairs. Outside the musicians were warming up; I
looked down toward the tent and saw a few navy umbrellas hurrying into the shelter.

I opened the drawer Mrs. Stoddard had gestured toward,
and looked at the scarves folded in neat squares, piled on top of
each other; then I closed it again and walked over to sit at her
dresser and look in her mirror. I took my hair out of the tight
ponytail I had combed it back into for lack of a better hairdo,
and I combed it out with her brush so that it fell loosely over my
shoulders. I looked through her lipstick until I found a bright
red one and screwed it up until the creamy tip was high out of
the shell. When I pressed it to my lips it came out thick and
glossy, and I puckered in the mirror like a movie star and blinked

my father's doleful eyes. The orchestra began to st[r]
below. I smiled at myself and stood to look in th[e]
mirror.

I did a little twirl to watch my skirt flare up and l[...]
over to where Mr. Stoddard's ties hung above a neat [...]
shoes. I stroked them like a harp and one fell loosely to the [...]
By the time I went back down the stairs I was feeling glamo[r...]
again, my hair down and my arms strong and graceful, my sh[oes...]
making a clip-clop on each step.

Out the window of my bedroom I could see umbrellas fun-
neling in under the tent, now dripping with heavy rain. I stripped
off my stockings and put them back into their egg-shaped box. I
put the box on the pillow but then changed my mind and put it
in the wastepaper basket I'd been staring at the night before,
which was decorated with a message written in yachting flags.
I slipped off the dress and tucked it back into my knapsack. I
found the T-shirt and sweater I had worn on the train and put on
my jeans. The music stopped and then started up again. I looked
out to see water pouring merrily off one corner of the tent. I
wrote Nate a note and put it on his pillow upstairs.

Dear Nate,
I've decided to take the train home. Thank you for inviting
me. I'm sorry I wore the wrong dress.

Yours, Miranda

I practically leapt out the front door into the rain. The driveway was packed with cars and flooded all the way back to the
bridge. I ran down the grassy bump in the middle, jumping to

the side whenever it went under water, until my sneakers were soaked and I ran blindly into the puddles. Soon my jeans were soaked too, cold and heavy as metal against my thighs, but I kept running. A heron started up from the marsh beside me, making a faulty takeoff into the strong wind, and even as it left me behind, still running, clumsy and soaked, I felt myself somewhere up in the air with it, my powerful shoulders aching, the rain and bright marsh below me.

27

The trains were running behind because of the storm, and I had to wait a couple of hours in the station. It was neat and sterile, and there was no place to buy anything hot to drink. I did my best to warm myself under the hand dryer in the women's room. I watched for Nate at the door to the station as darkness descended, and began to count the minutes: I knew I had done something that I could not take back. For one giddy moment, it had seemed like a choice—like freedom—and then it was merely the way things were, running in the soaking rain.

I was the only one getting on the train when it came. The lights in the carriage were dim, but it was warm, and most of the passengers were reading cozily, talking in murmurs. I went straight to the dining car and bought two cups of coffee. I drank them slowly, one cup after another, and after a while I felt my mind speed forward with the momentum of the train. I watched as the backs of houses ticked by, one sleepy life after another, the lit-up kitchen windows, the bicycles left out in the rain. Nate would have long since discovered I was gone; people would already be drunk and dancing. I tried to imagine him making the best of it, but the thought of his reading my stupid note, alone in his room, made me look with panic at the darkness out the window, praying for the city to reappear.

I got out Ana's address and phone number as soon as the train pulled into Grand Central. It never occurred to me to call her; instead, I got into a taxi and passed the paper through the hole in the Plexiglas. He nodded and passed it back. It was still raining, and the city was rushing with cars, only a few people on the sidewalks. Ana's block was relatively deserted when we got uptown; I rang her bell and after a few minutes I heard a voice crackling in Spanish over the intercom.

"It's Miranda," I said, trying not to sound desperate. "I'm looking for Ana?"

The intercom was quiet. I checked the address again. What if they hadn't understood me? What if she was up there and someone else had answered? Would they tell her I was here? I turned and looked out the smudged glass entry door at the street. Two boys biked furiously past, leaning into the rain, their sweatshirt hoods pulled up over their heads. I was debating whether to ring again, deciding I had simply rung the wrong bell, when she appeared at the bottom of the stairs. She smiled when she saw me, shaking her head.

"Hey," she said, opening the door with a brief glance back into the lobby. "What are you doing here?"

"I—I just got back," I said, trying to sound casual.

She rolled her eyes, though she looked pleased. "You almost woke everyone up," she said. "I'm babysitting."

"Sorry," I said.

"That's okay," she said. She looked down at the floor. "I can't—I mean they're not going to be back for another couple hours, but—" she smiled, already changing her mind. "I mean we gotta be careful."

"Okay," I said, grinning.

We stayed separate as we climbed the stairs, our faces blank, too giddy to look at each other. It had come right back the minute she let me inside—that full, pure excitement—that secret feeling, throbbing inside us while the rest of the world stayed quietly oblivious, closed doors, beaten up stairways, and ourselves, full of crazy, glowing light. She put her finger to her lips as she let me into her apartment and went to listen for a minute outside the bedroom where the children slept before she came back to me. We were too shy at first to kiss.

She went to get beers from the kitchen. The television was on in Spanish, a low murmur which Ana said helped the kids to sleep. We sat down on the couch. We took a few sips of beer.

She'd gotten in trouble for coming home so late on Thursday. "It's not like my sister doesn't do it all the time," she said, with a flash of resentment, "but I guess I usually—call ahead or whatever." She glanced shyly down at her beer.

I smiled, not sure if she was being modest or just blustering. I wasn't sure if she knew, either—it always seemed as if she was just making her whole self up right in front of me. I couldn't take my eyes off her: the way she leaned back on the couch like she knew I was watching, flexing her shoulders, and then the next minute picking at her beer label, too shy to talk. I kissed her but I could tell she was nervous with the kids sleeping; "Gun shy," she said.

"How'd everybody like the dress?" she finally asked.

I shrugged. "I didn't really end up wearing it," I said.

"Why not?"

"They—they wanted me to wear a shawl over it."

"Really?" She laughed, looking at me. "Whose wedding was it, anyway?"

"Well, that guy, Nate—"

"Your boyfriend?"

"Yeah—I mean it was his sister's wedding." I glanced up apologetically. "He wanted me to wear his mother's shawl."

"Weird," she said, her amusement waning. "What did you do?"

"I just left," I said, taking a casual swig of my beer.

"Without going to the ceremony or anything?"

"Well, I left him a note."

"A *note?*" she glanced over toward the bedrooms and then looked back at me in disbelief. "What did you say, sorry I ruined your sister's wedding?"

I looked down at the floor, my stomach turning. "I just said sorry I wore the wrong dress," I said quietly.

She was quiet. "He must be pretty mad," she said finally.

"I guess so."

"I would be." She took a sip of her beer.

"I know," I said, my eyes still glued to the carpet. "It wasn't very nice."

"And you're supposed to be the nice girl," she said, half-heartedly.

"I didn't really want to go in the first place."

"Well, maybe you could have told him that earlier," she said, her voice a little more gentle. "Like when he invited you."

"I know," I said.

"You're a little crazy," she said, smiling at last. "Aren't you?"

"I guess so," I said, even though it hadn't felt that crazy. "I don't really understand why weddings matter so much," I added, sounding petulant. I felt like something was gone between us; she had made me feel bad. Suddenly I wanted to go home. "Maybe I should go," I said, standing up.

She stood up too. Somehow we'd both been hurt. We weren't really looking at each other. "Will you be okay getting home?" she asked.

"Yeah," I said. I picked up my knapsack, too miserable to really think, anxious to get out of there. "I'll see you later," I said, when she let me out the door. She stood inside; it wasn't safe to kiss anyway.

It wasn't until I'd gotten to the bottom of the stairs and let the door to her building close behind me that I realized I should have asked her how to get a cab. They weren't exactly filling the streets. I didn't even know where the subway station was. I turned left and started down the block. The rain had stopped and the sidewalks looked clean under the streetlights; the heavy air had lifted. Inside the apartment buildings televisions flickered blue, the yellow light from the deli awning on the corner looked cozy. A low thudding bass started up behind me, filling the air until the car finally passed, the sound gushing out onto the sidewalk. Ahead of me three boys, wide apart on the sidewalk, walked a thick-necked dog on a leash.

Two men came out of the deli just as I approached, taking in the new air. They stopped talking to watch me go by. I had planned on stopping in, to ask directions to the subway, but I kept walking. I knew I should stop. I had Ana's phone number, I remembered, and I could always use a pay phone, ask her where the subway was. But instead I went stubbornly forward. I knew how to take care of myself. I had been fine without Ana; I had been fine without this city. At home I could steer straight through the dark to the cove when my father's light was out, I could take the dory across in the thickest fog.

I was walking fast, and had started to catch up to the boys with the dog when they stopped to talk to two young girls idling in a doorway with a small child. I felt them watching me as I hurried past, purposeless. It was a familiar feeling, anyway—being alone. I hadn't meant to expect more. It had just happened, as if it were a part of growing up, wanting to be with another person. When actually it wasn't, when actually it only got harder, being with other people—pleasing them, disappointing them.

I started to cry. It was stupid, I told myself, not knowing where I was going, but I didn't want to stop. And anyway there was a bigger avenue ahead, dim but rushing with cars; there would be a subway or a taxi there. It was just that I had never felt it before, that someone could be so close, like all you had to do was touch them, and they could see your life around them as if it were real, as if all the things you'd ever thought had made sense.

My father must have known, I thought, walking along the big avenue now, toward what looked like a bus stop—that I would fail at this, and come home. He must have known that I was like him, and that in the end we were best left alone. I sat on the bench until a bus came, and when I got on the driver told me he was going downtown. It was bright inside, and a man slept on a seat near the back. An empty bottle rolled in and out of the aisle beside him, in pace with our starts and stops, all the way through the city.

It was late when I got back to the institute, but the kitchen light was on, which usually meant that Walter and Robert were still out. I went straight upstairs and with a kind of dull determination got out my father's duffel bag and began to pack all my clothes. I sorted out the drawings all over the desk, lilies and daisies and jagged, fussy carnations, stems and leaves and shadowy beginnings. They seemed to me then another expression of my stupid uncertainty. I felt terrible. Exhaustion came over me like a spell. I felt chilled. I took off my clothes and curled up under the blankets. I would leave first thing in the morning, I told myself.

The phone began to ring down the hall the instant I closed my eyes. In all the weeks I'd been there, I had never answered the phone. I listened to it ring and ring like I was listening to a dream. It stopped and then it began to ring again.

Finally I got out of bed, and, wrapped in a towel, I made my way down the hall. When I got to Walter and Robert's door it stopped again. I stood very still. I could hear nothing but the empty house. I suppose I felt then like I had pushed open every door; I couldn't tell which were real, or where I had already been. Walter and Robert's door wasn't locked, and I guess it never had been. I walked into a large living room, which must have been directly over the library. It faced the street, and though the ceilings were lower, it had the same oddly affected grandeur as the rest of the house, with Robert and Walter's presence a secondary layer, as if, for the twenty-odd years they had lived there since Arthur died, they had been afraid to settle in. The only exception might have been the large television set in the hearth, like the toaster set on top of the stove in the kitchen. Someone had left a pair of shoes in front of it, which were carefully draped with a crumpled pair of gray socks. Robert, I decided.

Evidence of Walter was everywhere else—in the forgotten piles of books and papers, the ill-suited file cabinet in the corner, the jacket about to fall off the arm of a chair. The old mantel was full of framed photographs, with a few unframed ones of Robert and him propped timidly in front of them. The same photo my father had at home of Arthur and him in front of the institute was there too, in a thick silver frame; there were others of Arthur standing in groups, and one of my father and him standing in front of a large domed building. My father was smiling, his face giving nothing away.

I didn't know what I was looking for until I found it: a black and white photograph, in a thin wooden frame, of a young man wearing tight swim shorts. He seemed to be on a kind of outcrop, with sky all around him, an ocean nearby. He had his hands on his hips, his hair wet and slicked back, and he was squinting against the sun.

The phone began to ring again. I took the photo out from behind the other pictures to look at it more closely. It was my father, fresh from a swim, feeling handsome and young. He was even tanned, or so it seemed, his young skin softened by the gray tones of the photograph. I looked at every inch of him—his narrow, boyish torso, his small hips, his lean legs, his bare feet. He was not smiling, but it was the happiest I had ever seen him—intensely alive, bare, breathing.

The phone stopped, and then began to ring again. I went into the bedroom to watch it ring, holding the picture against me, and when it stopped I looked around the room. The bed was unmade. I found myself staring at the comforter, thrown messily over to one side, the pale blue fitted sheet underneath. The sunken pillows were disarranged. Three loose wrinkles shot across the blue surface to a soft depression where the last person had heaved himself up.

"Aren't you supposed to be in Connecticut?" said a voice behind me.

I turned around to find Robert, leaning against the doorway, his jacket slung characteristically over his shoulder.

"I came back," I said.

"I see that."

"I'm going home tomorrow," I said.

He looked at me curiously. "Did something happen at the wedding?"

"I just left," I said, still clutching the photograph, my towel. "It wasn't very nice." The phone began to ring again and I didn't move.

"I take it you'd rather I didn't get it?"

I shook my head.

He stood there with me, listening to the phone ring a few more times, and then he sighed and came forward into the room to quietly hang his coat in the closet. "Sounds like you could use a drink," he said, looking at me. "I was just about to have one myself."

I followed him, still holding on to everything as he walked back into their living room. He held up a bottle of whiskey, and when I nodded he took two glasses from the cabinet by the television and filled them halfway. I sat in an armchair and he sat on the couch. The whiskey tasted miraculously warm, and I felt so grateful I was ready to tell him everything. But he spoke first.

"It's very chaotic, isn't it," he said, tilting the whiskey to admire it, "when you are first in love."

"I guess," I said. He smiled at me sympathetically and it occurred to me that he had had a few other drinks besides the one we were sharing.

"I'm afraid I haven't made this a very easy time for you," he said, leaning back on the couch.

I shrugged, by way of agreement. "I'm not really that easy myself," I said.

"I was there, you know, when your father and Arthur met," he said, as if he hadn't heard me. "We used to go this bar together, and your father showed up alone one night. Everyone looked straight in those days but your father looked absolutely hopeless, and I dared Arthur to offer him a drink. Of course it helped that he was ridiculously good-looking, and then he had that accent, but anyway, Arthur just—well he just fell in love." He looked over at me and I smiled uncomfortably, not sure where this was going.

"You probably know, of course, that Arthur hired him," he went on, "and they went around Europe together looking for ancient books. I suppose Arthur was no angel, but in any case we all knew your father—or thought we did. I mean it wasn't like other men didn't have families. But anyway, Arthur got sick, and when he died he gave your father that island of his—which was fine—and then suddenly your father just disappeared, with that secretary or whatever, and never said a word to us. Until this summer, when he decided it might be convenient for you to visit."

I put down my drink. "I'm sorry if my father hurt your feelings," I said. A quiet, fierce loyalty had lit up inside me, as if he'd struck a match.

He blinked at me in surprise, and I stood up, still holding the picture. It seemed right suddenly that I should have it. That secretary was my mother and that heartbroken man was my father. I loved them both so profoundly that it had taken me my life to recognize it.

"I hope I haven't offended you," Robert said, looking up at me disingenuously from his place on the couch.

"I appreciate your concern," I said, smiling at him. My father's sarcasm had rescued me at last. Before he could say another word I turned and walked out the door, flooded with rage.

It was no wonder my father had disappeared. The whole world seemed full of hurt feelings and apologies, endless selfishness and explanations. Wasn't there anything that anyone could understand about each other? Weren't there some hurt feelings that mattered more? Or did it all matter just as much, interminably, wound after wound? I put the picture of my father down on my desk, looking at the sun all over him—his easy invulnerability, his confidence—and started to cry. I got into bed and curled up under the covers, crying for everything we'd lost, crying for everything I'd misunderstood, crying like I could swim in the sound of it, an ocean all around me.

28

When I woke in the morning I could smell the aftermath of the storm, the rain and leaves and sooty air, and I could think of nothing but seeing Ana again. My father's picture was on the desk; his duffel bag was filled with all my clothes. I lay in the bed and listened to the fragile quiet inside, the distant rush and screech of the Sunday morning city, trying to think.

Her family, of course, would be home on a Sunday morning. They would have breakfast together, I was sure, and she had said something about her mother occasionally dragging them all to church. I could call her, I thought, but her sister might answer, and what if she didn't want to speak to me? I considered waiting until the next day, when I could catch her in the cart again, but I had no wish to speak to Robert, and eventually Nate would call, if he hadn't already, or even come back to find me. In the end I decided to call from a pay phone near the institute once I'd left—I would ask if she could meet me somewhere, and if she said no, I would offer to come to her house.

She told me later that when I walked outside that morning and closed the institute door behind me I looked as if I would stop for no one. She was sitting on a stoop two doors down, smoking, and I didn't see her until I was right in front of her. She smiled when I stopped.

"I was just about to call you," I said, confused.

"Yeah?" she said, leaning back to have a look at me.

"Yeah," I said, suddenly afraid to look back at her. "I'm sorry I was so weird last night."

"Me too," she said. She sat forward and glanced down the street. "I think I was pissed about your stupid boyfriend," she said. She looked up at me, squinting in the sun. "But I guess he's pretty well taken care of now."

"I guess so," I said, sheepish.

She offered me a cigarette and when she lit it I sat down beside her. The sun felt good. "I was thinking maybe we could go for a drive," she said.

"I was thinking about going home," I said.

"To Maine?" She turned to me and her eyes met mine. "Yeah," I said. I wanted to kiss her and I could tell she wanted to kiss me. We started to smile again. "I think you should come," I said.

"You do?" she said, grinning now.

"Yeah," I said, and I kissed her, and she kissed me back, and we were kissing in the sun. Afterward we both sat back. I forgot about my cigarette until she took a drag of hers.

"How long's the drive, anyway?" she said.

When I told her she rolled her eyes. "I'll take you up there," she said, "if you promise you'll come back."

"Okay," I said, even happier.

She told her mother that Maria was leaving town and had asked her to stay in her apartment; she called the garage and told them her mother was sick; we bought a map of the East Coast and two big cups of coffee and an hour later we were headed up I-95. We whizzed past all the signs for the towns I'd seen from the train on the way to Nate's house; we went through Providence and then Boston, playing our music and smoking cigarettes in the anxious local traffic. The sun had set by the time we finally crossed the state line into Maine, and as we got farther from Portland the dark stretch of trees on either side of the highway grew deeper, the air cooler.

"What do you do all day," she asked, "when you live at the end of the earth?"

I'd never been able to sustain much of a conversation about my father's work—interest usually flagged the minute I explained that he was translating a book already written by a poet who had died two thousand years ago. But something about the dark, evergreen air reminded me of the year after Mr. Blackwell had left us, when my father and I were caught in Ovid's spell. I told her how my father used to read to me; I told her how for a while I had lived in a world in which trees spoke and gods flew, and how I thought that if I waited long enough things would get marvelous like they did in the stories Ovid told, and become something else.

"But the thing is they're not really happy stories," I said. "I mean when I think of them now I realize they're really about people who can't change, like my father, because they are too overwhelmed by the way they feel, and that's why all the magic happens, because they can't change, and something just explodes."

"But then aren't they happier?"

"I don't think so," I said, lighting a cigarette. "I used to think so, but now I think maybe they stay the same. Or anyway, Ovid's stories aren't really about what it's like to be changed. They're about how hard it is before you change, when everything feels like it's going to explode, or it has exploded, and you can't put together any of the pieces."

"But isn't that kind of like being in love?" Ana said.

I looked over at her, startled, and she smiled at me, like she was watching me learn.

I got us all the way into town though I'd never driven it, and straight to the dock, as if I'd meant to jump in the water. She stopped the van and we got out and stumbled into the pre-dawn darkness. I walked to the end of the pier, the boats on the dock moving gently around us, alive like they are in the dark. The island was barely visible, a small, dark mass against the bigger islands.

"It's freezing," she said, coming to stand beside me.

I pulled her in, wrapping my arms around her with my chest against her back. "If you look," I said, "you can see the island, a little darker against the sky."

"Are you going to swim?" she said, leaning back against me as I wrapped her tight again.

"I don't know," I said. "I didn't really think that far ahead."

I kissed her on the cheek and she turned around and kissed

me on the mouth. "Let's go back to the van and think about it," she said, taking my hand and turning me around.

It was cold outside, I realized, as soon as we got back to the van, which was still warm from the heat we'd had on for the last few hours of the trip. I went into the back to get my sweaters out of my duffel bag and by the time I'd found them she had dozed off in the front seat. I tucked the sweaters on top of her and gave her a kiss and then put on my old jacket and sat in my own seat to watch the sky lighten. Before long the fishermen pulled into the parking lot at the breakwater. I watched them getting out of their trucks, carrying cups of coffee, coolers of food, talking as they pulled their boots from the front seats of their trucks, some of them already in their coveralls. They went down to the dock in twos and threes and before long they were motoring out into the channel in the half-dark, the water shimmering under their mast lights and shaking apart in their glittering wakes.

Mr. Blackwell and some of the other fishermen kept old dinghies tied up on a slip at the gas dock, and once most of the boats were out I went down to see if Mr. Blackwell's was there. It was the only one without a touch of rainwater in the bilge, the oars stowed neatly. One summer everyone had kept their oars stowed in their trucks, because a tourist had taken Bob Haskin's boat and tipped it. But they'd put them back. It occurred to me that was the way people in Yvesport always were—stubbornly trusting, like they were daring you to change. And Mr. Blackwell wasn't any different, I thought, as I went back up the metal ramp, gripping the cold, familiar railing. That was half the reason I loved him.

Ana was still asleep, her face buried in the brown wool sweater I'd tucked around her shoulders. I kissed her and told her I would pick her up on the dock in an hour, and she looked confused.

"I have to go over to the island to get the boat," I explained.

She looked at me, her face still soft with childish puzzlement, and I felt a surge of love sweeping through me like sadness. I kissed her again on her warm forehead, my eyes suddenly full of tears.

"I'll come back and get you," I whispered, overwhelmed, but she was already hunkering back into her own warmth, mumbling assent.

I had never rowed across, but Mr. Blackwell had done it as if it was nothing whenever he couldn't use the *Sylvia B.* I could see the island now; already the sunrise had begun to pink through the trees around the cove, the sky above it opaque, a cloudy white, like the inside of an old quahog shell.

I pushed myself away from the dock and the oarlocks rattled as I took my first awkward strokes, my shoulders stretching stiffly as the boat lurched forward and the water grasped at the oars. It was choppy once I got out of the harbor into the channel, and little waves slapped and shook the fragile old hull. My hands had begun to burn a little from the cold, but soon I'd passed the channel marker and knew I was more than halfway. I looked over my shoulder to mind the rocks as I rowed into the cove.

Our house, up on the hill, looked smaller and quieter than I remembered. I had always thought of the path from the shore as a long uphill, with tall trees backing it in a dense protective wall.

They were tall but scrappy with fall undergrowth, and the house hid shyly amongst them. The smoke of a newly lit fire puffed out of the crooked chimney. The porch my father and Mr. Blackwell had built was actually in tender proximity to the drop of the rocky beach and our modest pier, where the two boats were kept.

I tied up the dinghy, feeling strangely exposed on the dock. I thought I saw my father's shadow passing by a window as I started up the path, and I told myself it was just the sunlight moving with me, but I couldn't shake the feeling that I was intruding, and that somehow I didn't belong. Maybe he is the one who has changed, I thought. Maybe he will be like this house, unexpectedly worn and small.

But when he opened the door there he was: tall and stooped, his sweet white hair uncombed, the bottom of his sweater just coming unraveled.

"I saw you rowing in," he said, his eyes shining.

I felt in a strange panic that he should close the door to keep the warmth from going out, and then suddenly I felt my own throat close with tears. I had had this feeling, from the day I left, that somehow he knew where I was, but of course he hadn't—he hadn't known where I was at all.

I sort of rushed at him, and kissed the skin of his bare neck, pressed my face into his shoulder. All along I had been imagining him here, making himself dinner, writing at his desk, and here he was, just as I thought. He put his arms around me and held me tight, and I thought how very much I loved him, how maybe I had never loved him so much.

When we finally let go, he blinked and cleared his throat. "I was just—making some coffee," he said unsteadily, stepping back in his slippers to let me in.

The house was full of everything I remembered, the ragged wall of manuscripts, the sea lavender I'd hung to dry two years earlier, the kettle I had scrubbed to shining before I left. I felt the creak of the floorboards under my feet, looked out the window at the water, as if it too was part of the house, part of us.

He filled two mugs with coffee in the kitchen and took them out to the table with the sugar bowl, like I was a guest. "You're drinking it black?" I asked him nervously, noticing he hadn't added any cream to his.

"Oh, yes," he said, smiling. "There've been some big changes around here." He pushed the sugar at me. "I'm out of milk, actually," he said, wincing at his first sip.

I laughed and touched the chips around the edge of my mug with my finger. We were both quiet.

"You should have written," he said. "I didn't know you were coming."

"I didn't really plan—anything," I said.

He looked at me, and I tried to smile, but I was afraid I would cry again. "How are you liking the city?" he asked gently.

I swallowed. "I like it," I said, as if the fact that I would return was already a given. How had it come to seem so complicated?

"I liked it myself," he said. He was looking at me the way he always did, with perfect seriousness.

I smiled at his certainty, not sure why it surprised me. I think I had always known he had loved New York, just as I had always known that there were times in his life when he had been happier. I felt as if I no longer knew what it was that I felt he had hidden from me—what I meant to ask him, what I didn't already know.

"I'm thinking of going to art school," I announced, as if I'd suddenly grown up.

He nodded. "I would imagine you'd have quite a few choices in the city."

"There are a few public ones, if you live there."

"You may have to find a way to earn a living," he said, a little apologetically. "But it's not a bad city for that, is it?"

"No," I said smiling. "I'm a pretty good typist, anyway."

"Were Walter and Robert kind enough?"

I hesitated. "They were pretty busy." I took a sip of my coffee. "I guess Robert was pretty jealous of you and Arthur," I added boldly.

My father looked up at me. I wished instantly that I could take it back, but he was already stung. It seemed as if I had simply dropped out of his vision. He looked down at the table, like he was searching through a fog.

"I love you," I said, suddenly.

He looked back at me. "I know you do," he said with a weary smile. "I love you too."

It is astonishing, in the end, how difficult it is to know the things you know. What I mean is that all I had discovered was everything I knew all along. I don't know when we'd ever told each other how much we loved each other, but suddenly I couldn't see why I had ever doubted it. He took a sip of his coffee and for a minute—only a minute—I saw how astonishingly handsome he was. It was just long enough to take in his wide, dark eyes, the stone smoothness of his cheeks, his gently curved mouth—the man he had been all his life: that superior kind of beauty that never belongs. And then he was my father again, sitting across from me, holding on to his coffee mug as if it might slip off the table.

Acknowledgments

Many thanks to the MacDowell Colony, where this book started, and Yaddo, where it sputtered along. This book would never have been written without the support of many loyal friends and readers, including, among many others: Sydney Blair, Julie Crawford, Liza Darnton, Deborah Draving, Nell Eisenberg and Deborah Eisenberg, Matthew Engelke, Leslie Falk, Sophie Fels, Jane Fleming, Christina Kiely, Heather Love, David McCormick, Ana Moran, Brenna Munro, Rebecca Nash, Andrea Schaefer, Lara Shapiro, Hilary Steinetz, Maria Striar, Sarah Sze, Amy Williams, and finally, Inez Murray, who keeps me steady.